A Wedding in Somewhere

Somewhere, TX

Book #3

Emma Roman

KC Klein

Lavender Daye

Jodi Vaughn

Becca Boyd

Krystal Shannan

R.L. Syme

Table of Contents

Chapter One
by Emma Roman

July 4, 2015 – 6 a.m.

The Saddles for Hope parking lot was a war zone. Chunks of the hay bales lay in a charred messy pile. Michael Torez parked his truck and slammed the door. They'd painstakingly stacked that hay wall only the day before.

He stood near the bed of his truck, waiting while the other stable hand parked, too.

Jeremy rounded his truck, shrugged and grunted toward the mess, while shoving the remainder of a large breakfast burrito into his mouth.

"I know," Michael said. "Anna's gonna flip a switch when she sees this, if she hasn't already." He pointed toward the gaping hole in the large hay wall near the horse barn.

The Kane wedding was the talk of the town and they'd worked hard for those crazy wedding planners the last few days, setting up the hay bales, chairs, tables, decorations, and everything else that needed to be prepped for the ceremony today.

Eggs and bits of tortilla spewed from his buddy's mouth. "Shit! I didn't see that yet. What happened? Did they try to burn the whole place down?"

Michael kicked a toaster-sized chunk of hay near his foot and frowned. "This shit is wet."

"That's why it's in on the concrete parking lot, dude. At least whoever put out the fire knew that much."

"Still, they shouldn't have just left it here."

Jeremy raised his arms over his head and stretched, rolling his neck from one side to the other. "You want me to get the tractor? Or just use one of our trucks? Or go wake up the boss and see what she wants us to do?" He waggled his eyebrows and grinned. "She's always so cute in the morning."

Michael shook his head. Anna Granger was *not* cute when she woke up. He'd seen her early in the morning, and if she didn't have her coffee thermos half-downed already, she was someone you wanted to avoid. Jeremy just had the hots for her. A crush always blinded a person from seeing faults. Anna could've worn a burlap sack and Jeremy would still think she was sexier than the most popular movie star.

"Let's at least try and fix this damn wall before any of the wedding people show up. We can pull some bales from the top and fill in the hole they knocked out," Michael said, taking charge. "I'll try and get a hold of those wedding planner ladies. I've got their numbers in an email from Anna. Hopefully they won't freak at the *adjustments*." He pulled out his phone and dialed the first number on the list. Straight to voicemail.

"We still have to move some from the ends, or it's gonna be uneven," Jeremy argued. "Like a shark took a bite right out of the middle."

Michael finished the message to Claire Milton, then turned back to Jeremy. "There are no sharks in Texas. And we can taper it on the ends so it looks more natural. Come on. Get in my truck. We'll go around to the back side of the pavilion and swipe some from there first."

They worked at the speed required to finish before any horrified wedding planners arrived on the ranch, or their boss woke for the morning.

After taking a few bales from one end of the wall, they unloaded them from the bed of Michael's truck, pushing and pulling until the replacements fit into the middle of the offset stacked bales perfectly.

"We didn't get enough," Jeremy groaned, wiping sweat from his forehead with the back of his gloved hand.

Michael stared at the wall. It needed at least seven or eight more bales to hide the fact that it'd been destroyed only hours before. If they took more from the pavilion side though, it would really start to show.

"Some from the front end?" he asked, pointing up the road.

Jeremy nodded, climbing into the bed of Michael's truck and sitting. He patted the side. "Let's go."

Michael jogged to the driver's door, climbed in and pulled up next to the edge of the wall. Jeremy grabbed the bales they needed and Michael backed up to the still-halfway-gaping hole in the middle of the wall.

He slid out of the truck and hurried to the open tailgate, helping Jeremy move the oversized bales from the bed to the stacked wall as quickly as possible. The sun was starting to rise and they had only a few minutes left before the stable manager, Peter Gibson, showed up and Anna emerged from her cabin just up the road.

"Hey look," Jeremy said, pointing up the road.

Michael turned. A large fire engine was barreling down the long drive toward them, flashing their lights. *What the hell?*

He waved his hand at the big red engine and turned back to Jeremy. They shoved the last bale into place, finally patching the massive hole. The ends would look like stairs, but there was nothing they could do about that.

"Boys!"

Both stable hands turned toward the angry voice. Will Johnson was stomping his way across the parking lot. The grimace on his face foretelling a doom worse than talking to Anna before she'd had her coffee.

"Shit, he looks pissed," Jeremy whispered before jumping .

"You think!" Michael spat back.

He followed Jeremy and they both stood silently together, waiting to hear how this catastrophe was going to be their fault. Everything was *always* their fault. But this guy didn't look like the kind who smacked them upside the head like Peter did when they messed up and then went on his way—everything forgiven.

"What are you doing to my crime scene?" His face was red and the veins in his neck bulged, pulsing angrily.

"Geez," Jeremy groaned.

"No way, mister," Michael called out, refusing to get blamed for something that wasn't even close to their fault. "There was no tape. No nothing that said this was a crime scene. We were just trying to clean up," he said, taking a step forward. "There's a wedding here in a few hours and I don't know about you, but pissed off wedding planners, brides, and bridesmaids are way more frightening than you."

The fireman scowled, but didn't yell again.

Michael sighed, maybe they really would get out of this without being smacked or blamed. Not that it wasn't usually their fault they were always getting into trouble.

It would still be a nice change for once to not be the ones causing the chaos.

Chapter Two
by KC Klein

Brent decided he'd risk it. He took a deep breath, braced himself, then raised his head and cracked open an eyelid.

Mistake—gray concrete walls and cold, steel bars swirled past his vision. With the utmost care, he laid his head back down. He'd seen enough. It took a moment, but it was amazing how the memory of the town's holding cell came flooding back. This wasn't his first trip to the Long Rock County Jail. He'd made a few overnight stays in his misspent youth—most of the time Derrek was sitting next to him yelling about how Brent, or TJ Stinson, had to stop coming up with one stupid idea after another. But this time a quick sideways glance, one that didn't involve moving his head, showed he was alone.

Brent's stomach lurched as he concentrated on drawing in several deep breaths through his nose until he could open his eyes without vomiting. What was Derrek's cure for a hangover again? Two raw eggs and some NyQuil? The image had Brent turning over on the small cot with a groan, but it was more than just a night of drinking that was weighing on him.

Okay, think Brent. Besides a wicked hangover, something else was wrong. Something important was gnawing on him.

What gave you the first clue, idiot? The fact that you're in jail?

Jail? *Jail.* How the hell had he ended up in jail? Brent closed his eyes and tried hard to probe his memory of anything that could have landed him here.

Yes, the bachelor party. That had gone off pretty smooth. He and a few

4

of his friends had gone out. Okay, more like twenty guys. Well, a bit more if one counted all the people who happened to be at Joe's Bar at the time, but regardless it had started off simple enough.

They'd had dinner at Joe's, which was supposed to be followed by karaoke and a few beers. Beers he could handle. There was no way his ass was here because of a few beers. Brent rubbed at his aching head and tried to think back. And then there'd been some more beers… and maybe even a few shots of tequila, which explained the Mexican bandits yelping and shooting off rifles inside his head.

None of that should've landed him in jail. He wouldn't be much of a rock star if he couldn't handle a few beers and a couple of shots. That was all that'd happened. A simple celebration between friends until someone had ordered a round of The Black Liquorish of Death, aka the memory sweeper.

All kneel before the God of alcohol.

All hail the Jager.

His stomach did a solid one-eighty and a thin sheen of sweat broke out over his skin.

After the Jager bombs, all went fuzzy. Actually no, fuzzy insinuated that there was something there. Nope, his memory was *nada* , blank, zilch.

He swore.

Well, now ya gotta do it. Now, there's no hope for it except to go down the list and do the reality check.

Time for the tally.

Partying like a rock star was something of a badge of honor in the music industry—a prerequisite for a celebrity like him. As a survival strategy, he'd used a little trick of how to piece together the night before during the morning after.

Mentally, he conjured up an image of a piece of paper with a line down the middle. He put a plus sign on one side and a negative on the other. *Okay Brent, time for the clothes check.* He glanced down at himself, patted his belt buckle—still there and securely fastened. He smiled.

One mark for the positive.

He patted down his jeans, front and back pocket—no phone. No wallet.

One mark in the negative.

In jail. *Negative.*

Hung over. *Definite negative.*

About two seconds away from throwing up. *Negative. Negative.*

He'd never been great at math, but even he didn't need a calculator to figure out that his equation was a bit lopsided. Mentally, he went back up to having all his clothes on and gave himself two marks in the positive.

Gotta give credit where credit was due.

Feeling slightly better, Brent tried to piece together any reason he might've ended up here.

A few images flashed through his head—another round, a public restroom, and… ah few…um, strippers.

He groaned. He had no idea who called the strippers, but that was not something he wanted to explain to DJ.

His mind floated on the image of DJ. Her dark hair, her almond shaped eyes, her long sexy legs. God, how he loved her legs. And that's when he knew where his anxiety was stemming from.

DJ. DJ. DJ. His fiancée, the woman he was going to marry tomorrow. As in the day after his bachelor party.

A fresh wave of fear washed over him drowning out the previous nausea.

The wedding was tomorrow, right? Tomorrow as in the day after tonight.

What the hell time was it? He patted down his pants for his phone and came up empty handed—again.

He jumped up, not at all caring that the room still spun. "Hey, hey," he said, pressing his face flush against the cool metal bars. "Help, hey, I need my phone. Someone out there. I need my phone just for a minute."

"Quit making all that racket, boy, I'm trying to sleep," said a gruff voice from behind.

Brent whipped his head around which was a mistake. The movement almost brought him to his knees.

In the cell next to him, a rather large, dark-haired man sat up on his cot, hands braced on either side. His knees were almost to his ears as he maneuvered around the small bed, reminding Brent of the lazy grasshopper in the children's story about a hardworking ant.

He was surprised he hadn't noticed earlier, probably because he'd been too preoccupied with other things—namely congratulating himself on having kept his pants on.

The man looked up and scowled in his direction and Brent recognized him immediately. "Sheriff West. Thank God. You need to help me. I need to get out of here. I need my phone. I gotta call DJ, no Derrek. I gotta get home."

Randall West snorted while rubbing some of the sleep from his eyes. "Being in jail kinda prevents you from doing any of those things. One of the deterrents for coming to visit." The sheriff laughed at his own joke.

Brent didn't get it.

Randall sighed. "Look around, boy. I'm not sitting in this cell for my health."

Realization of the scope of his situation started to set in. Why the hell was the sheriff sitting in the cell next to him?

"Oh, don't look so dejected, boy," Randall said. "Not like it's personal and I got a phone shoved up my keester and I'm not letting you use it or anything."

Brent couldn't help his look of disgust at that mental image. *Thanks, buddy.* Probably wouldn't want to use it after that anyway. He tried a different angle. "What are you in here for anyways?"

Randall shrugged. "They brought me up on double homicide. Said I killed two people who woke me up from my nap."

With the look Randall gave him, Brent wasn't at all sure the sheriff was joking.

Then the old man broke his hard gaze and started to laugh. "Don't look at me that way. It's not like I really did it or anything."

The old coot had always been a little strange, and now this confirmed it. Brent had stepped into the twilight zone. He shuffled a bit farther to the opposite side of his cell, suddenly glad there were metal bars between them. "You don't understand. I have a wedding to get to tomorrow. I really need to get out."

"Oh, I understand. Everyone in this damn town knows about you and your wedding. But what you need to understand is that you're gonna have to convince Wally to let you go, since he was the one I saw brought you in last night. So good luck with that," Randall said with a dismissive flare that had Brent wondering how the man had ever won an election.

But there was one phrase that struck Brent causing the sudden pounding of his heart to make his head hurt a hell of a lot worse. "Did you say, last night?"

"Yep."

"As in, the morning after the night I was brought in?"

"Yep."

If today was tomorrow then that meant…Brent swallowed hard. "Are you saying that today is Saturday?"

"Been following Friday since God set up the seven day work week in Genesis."

Brent's aunt had always complained about menopause and the sudden hot flashes that would come out of nowhere. He never had any sympathy— until now. The sudden change in his body temperature from hot to cold and then hot again would've given Aunt Martha a run for her money. "What time is it?"

Randall shrugged one shoulder and then showed off his empty wrist. "Jackasses took my watch also, but I'm guessing around nine."

"In the morning?" He couldn't help the sudden rise in his voice's octave level.

The sheriff jerked back at Brent's yell. "Well, sure the hell isn't nine at night. I thought they taught kids how to tell time in school these days or is that not part of the "new math" they're teaching?"

Brent stared out of the bars, and glanced both ways down the empty hall. "There's been a mistake. I don't belong here. I...I..."

"Yeah, that's what they all say. Save it for the judge."

He gripped the bars to keep himself steady. "When is the judge coming?"

Randall awkwardly turned himself around and stretched out on the small cot, letting his booted feet hang off the edge. "Well, I think the judge likes to do some fishing on Saturday. Not really into working on the weekend. Then that takes us to the Sabbath, so yeah, not happening then. I'd say the earliest would be Monday. Maybe by noon if you're lucky. Tuesday if you're not."

His knees buckled, and he was glad the cot was close to keep him from falling on his butt. DJ was going to kill him.

Not just maybe. *Really*.

She'd been against having this big wedding from the beginning. She'd wanted something small at first, possibly at the ranch with just them and a few close family and friends. But nooooooooooo! Brent just had to go big. Had to go all out and the only way he finally convinced DJ was by telling her they would be doing Tande and Claire a favor by hiring them as their wedding planners to plan the most expensive wedding the town had ever seen. Apparently, Tande and Marcus's stint in the tabloids had really caused their company to take a hit.

A big wedding was something that Brent had wanted, but then Sally had gotten involved and if there was ever a way for his agent to create a publicity angle she took it. Why Brent had ever agreed to mixing a fan event with his wedding, he'd never know.

And now he wasn't even going to be there.

Just last night DJ had been stressing over all the things that had gone wrong—the threatening letters, the black roses, the bridesmaids dresses. She talked about wanting to pull the plug on the whole event and that maybe all these mishaps were signs from the Universe telling them not to get married. He didn't believe that for a moment. DJ was an answer to his prayers, and if God had all of a sudden wised up and changed His mind, that was of no concern to Brent. He'd been fortunate enough that she'd agreed to marry him in the first place. And if he didn't show up today, she'd never agree to it again.

He walked back over to the bars and started to rattle them as hard as he could. If he was annoying enough maybe they'd give him some attention. Pretty much the motto of his life. "Hey, hey, I need my phone call. I have rights. I have the right to know what charges I'm being held on. I have a right to know why I was arrested."

The noise hurt his head, but there was no help for it. He was now officially desperate enough to even try Derrek's hangover remedy.

"Brent? Brent Kane? Is that you?" said a sickly sweetened voice that was a bit too high pitched for Brent this early in the morning.

He looked around, trying to figure out where the voice was coming from. He glanced over at the sheriff who pointed to the cement block wall on the side of him.

"Yooo hoo! Down here." He saw a slender arm sticking out of what he assumed was another cell.

"It's us! Goldy Wilkes and Alice Lee. From your fan club."

Brent threw a questioning look over to the sheriff who shrugged. "Two crazies they picked up last night. Apparently, arrested for setting some hay bales on fire at the Saddles for Hope Ranch. Freaking loonies."

The Saddles for Hope Ranch? Where his wedding was going to being held? Holy—

"We love you, Brent. We love you. I'm your number one fan!"

"No, I'm your number one fan," said the other woman. He couldn't tell who was Goldy and who was Alice Lee.

"No, it's me."

"No, I am."

There was some shuffling around and then a loud ouch followed by a muffled curse. "Who's the president of his fan club? *Me.* I'm his number one fan."

"Only because you voted yourself in." Came the other woman's catty reply, and whose voice was only slightly less annoying. "Anyone can vote herself in as the president."

There was some more bickering, but Brent worked hard to block it out. He remembered those two only because they were hard to forget. They pretty much made themselves known whenever they were in his vicinity.

He should've eloped.

"Did you ladies actually set fire to the hay wall around where we're holding our reception?"

There was some awkward silence.

And then the litany was back. "We love you, Brent. We looooovvee you so much. Marry me and not *her.* I'll be your slave. I'll make you sooo happy."

He looked over at Randall who was nodding with a smirk on his face. "Now that one," he said, nodding his head toward the nuts on the other side of the wall, "wouldn't mind if you were two days late to your wedding. Maybe you should take her up on it."

Brent gritted his teeth. This was ridiculous. He was a rock star, for Christ's sake. He had people whose sole responsibility was to pick up his dry cleaning and fetch him a latte. He was pretty sure there was someone on his payroll who could take his place in jail until Monday. He just had to call Sally and ask. With renewed effort, he started rattling his cage again. "Heelloo Hello! I need a phone call. I demand a phone call!"

9

The door at the end of the hall finally opened, and a brown haired, plump faced man in a tan uniform poked his head in. "What the hell is all this racket about?"

"Now you did it," Randall chimed in, apparently nominating himself as the sole member of Brent's peanut gallery. "One more crazy in here and this place will be a certified loony bin."

Brent ignored him. "Hey, hi, oh, am I glad to see you. It's Wally, right? I need help. There's been some kind of mistake here. You've got the wrong person."

"Are you Brent William Kane?" The deputy strutted down the hall as if he was a noble man walking among his serfs.

No one but his mother had ever called Brent by his full name, but he nodded.

Wally crossed his arms over his thick middle and shook his head. "Then, not a mistake."

Brent threw up his arms. "What do you mean *not a mistake*? What did I do? Why am I under arrest? I demand to talk to my lawyer."

Wally made his way to stand in front of Brent. Close, but not close enough for Brent to reach out and clamp his hands around Wally's throat. Which was too bad, since he'd like nothing better than to wipe the smug grin off of Wally's face that said no one else but Wally knew the butt of the joke.

Well, that was obvious. *Idiot.*

"You know what you did. And I—" Wally jabbed his thumb to his chest "was the only one with enough balls to cross the line of fame and wealth and place you under arrest. The long arm of the law reaches everyone. Just 'cause you're some pretty faced rock star doesn't mean you can get away with running a prostitution ring."

"A what?!"

Randall let out a bark of laughter. "Oh, this is good. That pretty fiancée of yours is gonna looovvve this. Who says nothing interesting happens in Somewhere?"

"What did you say?" Brent couldn't have heard Wally right.

"Oh, they told me." Wally bobbed his head up and down as if he was tied to the end of a fishing pole. "You run one of the most profitable human trafficking rings in the whole southwest. Yep, I got it all figured out. You turn a nice tidy profit, and then launder it through your phony dance and pony show."

"No." Brent shook his head real slow. "I make money because I'm an actual country music star. Because I sing songs. I have fans. People buy my records."

"Oh, how original. Now, I guess you're going to tell me that your rock star biz is legit."

Brent blinked once. Twice. He wanted to make sure he was awake and not dreaming. "Yes…because it is."

"That's what they all say." Wally scrunched up his face and snorted. "Please, I've heard your music, you expect me to believe that people actually buy that crap?"

Okay, this was starting to feel like a rerun of his childhood. "You mean the album that went platinum? The one up for an Emmy? Yeah, I expect you to believe that people buy *that crap.*"

Yeah, he was pissed off enough that he had actually done air quotes.

"You have to admit that Emmy nomination was pretty surprising." This from the peanut gallery again.

"Really?" Brent said, not even turning around. "Not taking the opinion of a man here on a double murder charge."

"We love you, Brent," said the one he assumed was Goldy from up the hall. "We promise to write you every day in jail. No matter what, I'll still be your number one fan."

"She can be your number one fan, and I can be your conjugal visit girl," shouted Alice.

Brent dug at the pounding of his temples. Really, this how was this his life? He'd gladly take those two raw eggs and Nyquil now.

He took a deep cleansing breath, the type that Sally was always trying to get him to practice. Arguing with crazy would get him nowhere. Time to try a different tactic. "Okay, Okay, I'll make you a deal. I may be willing to help you out. You give me my phone call and I'll write you up a full confession."

Even still slightly drunk and wickedly hungover, Brent was pretty proud of himself. That was a good plan.

"Do you think I'm stupid?"

Brent wisely kept his mouth shut.

Of course, everyone else in jail would pick that moment to keep theirs shut also.

"Do you really believe I would think it would be that easy?" Wally narrowed his already tiny eyes until they seem to disappear into his pasty face altogether. The effect was unnerving. "That I would believe you would confess so quickly? Is that what you think I think?"

Actually, Brent had no idea what Wally was thinking. He was afraid if he ever peered inside Wally's head it would have the same effect as Medusa's hair and turn him to stone.

"Nope." Wally shook his head, continuing the conversation all by himself. Which was just as well, Brent was at a complete loss. "You just cool your heels for a bit and think about living with the fear of dropping the soap for the rest of your life."

Brent's mouth was still hanging open as he watched the deputy waddle out of the room. It took him a moment to realize that the fear chilling his blood wasn't over Wally's craziness—sooner or later, he had to encounter a sane person in the justice system—but is was recalling DJ's words to him last night.

"I swear Brent Kane, one more damn thing goes wrong with this wedding and I'm calling this whole thing off."

He wondered if she'd consider the groom not showing up to be that *one more damn thing?*

Chapter Three
by Becca Boyd

Will Johnson surged toward the reconstructed hay wall and the two young Saddles for Hope staff who held pitchforks in their hands. "What are you doing to my crime scene?"

The short one grimaced. "Geez."

"No way, mister. There was no tape, no nothing that said this was a crime scene." The other one came at him, almost aggressive. "We were just trying to clean up."

Will looked around while they blathered on about a wedding and a bride or some shit. He didn't have time for this.

"You're done cleaning. Get out of here." Will waved them off. They protested, but he ignored them. He'd chase them off if he had to. Will had shit to do.

Chief Shane had called Will at ungodly o'clock and ordered him to get back out and finish the investigation. *And for shit's sake, take the cops out there with you this time, Will.*

The siren of a cop car whooped at him and Will waved Eli over. There was another deputy in the passenger seat. Not Wally this time, thank the good Lord. That dude was dense.

"This is the third time I've been out at this ranch in two days." Eli groaned as he got out of the cruiser. "I could never see these grounds again and be all right."

Will stuck out his hand for a handshake, and Eli obliged.

"I'm with you there, man." Will pointed to the hay wall, then the pavement. "Boys on the ranch staff moved bales from each end to fix the hole in the middle, but I think all of the burned out stuff is here."

The sidekick came around the car and stared at them, silently. Eli picked up a handful of the hay. "Looks like you guys soaked this down pretty good."

Will kicked at a half-bale near his foot. "They pulled out all the wet stuff and left it on the pavement."

"Smart," Eli said. "Wet hay in this weather could be dangerous."

"We won't let it sit long enough." Will dug out his gloves. "Once we look at this, we'll let the new chief know if we should call the State Investigator or not."

"I thought those women confessed." The young ranch hand turned over another bale.

"Oh, they did." Will kept walking around the dregs. "The chief wants us to file a request about the Fire Investigators. Said one of the women called a lawyer, but I don't think so."

"The way I heard it," Eli said, "They couldn't wait to confess."

Will chuckled, remembering the strange scene with a bus of Brent Kane's fans and Marcus trying to arrest everyone. "That's the truth. One of them confessed quickly. The other one was…not as accommodating."

Deputy Sidekick moved a stack of hay with his foot. "They're only partially burned. What does that mean?"

They moved across the parking lot, looking at charred remnants until the bales were black lumps.

Will dug into one of them and the middle was still yellow. "It means they didn't burn for long."

"And what does that mean?"

"It means that Marcus's story holds up." Will smacked his hands together. "He said they saw the smoke right away and called 9-1-1. He was able to get part of the wall down before the fire spread far. Hay catches fast, but it burns slow. We put this out before it had burned very long."

"So it couldn't have sat burning for a long time," Eli finished.

Will looked around. "I guess we should do something official, though…"

A burst of static interrupted him. "All available units. Reported firearm discharge at the River Hotel. One-one-eight-seven Long Rock Road. Rescue unit responding. Please call in."

Eli slipped into the driver's seat. "Ruby, this is Eli. Can you repeat that?"

The radio screeched. Weekend daytime dispatch was Ruby Burke, and she had a Bayou accent that sometimes required two or three goes at the sentences before some of the Yankees like Eli could pick them up.

"Employees at the River Hotel reported a shooting, honey. Head on over there and call in when you can."

"Sorry, Will. We should get going." Eli jumped in and put his keys in the transmission. Sidekick followed like deputy dog and the two were back out onto Sweet Mountain Road before Will realized he'd been left by his only help.

Shooting? At the River Hotel? And the chief trying to stir up some shit with what should have been and open-and-closed case? *Hell.*

Will just wanted the low-key life that he'd always had. Party with a few buddies, maybe have a girl around for a while, watch some good football—and now, with that new kid at McA, some good basketball—and get his job done. No complications.

Good luck with that. Somewhere was fast turning into a town full of complications, and there was nothing Will could do to stop it.

"Hey, you boys," he called over to the stable hands. They stopped shoveling hay out of the back of the truck and looked up. "Come on over and clean all this up. This case is closed."

Chapter Four
by Lavender Day

The phone rang too damn early on a Saturday morning and Sherri London crawled over Hart to grab the receiver, giving him an eyeful and a twitch of *'what the hell, I'll die happy, along the way.'* He'd teach her the meaning of *back from Austin on vacation* when he could think straight.

"London B&B. How can I help you?"

One hand managed to free itself from the bed covers—at least, he planned to use that as an excuse when that hand made its way to Sherri's soft, sweet, and completely bare ass.

She flinched and shot a hot look his direction. "It's for you, Mr. Hart Winston."

He caught the phone in midair, thankful she threw like a girl. "I have seven days of vacation. Make it fast."

"My apologies about the disruption of your vacation, especially at such an early hour, but I need your help. Somewhere needs your help."

Hart looked at Sherri, wondering what she might've gotten him involved in, but she looked clueless. "Who are you?" he asked the man on the other end of the line. Hart held the phone out and switched it to speaker.

"County Commissioner Rufus Landry."

He raised a brow and Sherri confirmed the man's identity. "And what do you need me to do, Commissioner?"

"Ranger Winston, your investigations have put us in a bind here in Somewhere. We're in need of a Sherriff and we'd like to offer you the job."

Sherri shifted, sat up higher on the bed, and he could almost read her thoughts. She wanted him to take the job. He sure as hell didn't want to disappoint her.

"Commissioner, I'm a Texas Ranger, not a politician. Sherriff is an elected position."

"Our bylaws allow me to appoint someone to the position in this instance, and I'm quite sure the citizens of Somewhere would be happy to have a former Texas Ranger at the helm of our law enforcement team."

The smoke the commissioner blew—even over the phone—didn't change Hart's convictions. "As a ranger, I can assist in the short term and advise as needed. Not exactly how I'd like to use my vacation, but I'll do it if you need me. As for the job, I'll have to say no."

The commissioner stammered for a few minutes, offering incentives and whatnot, but all Hart could focus on was the expression on Sherri's face. Hell, her whole body was rigid. "Sorry, but I'm a Texas Ranger, not a politician." He disconnected the call and turned to Sherri.

And the storm brewing in her eyes.

"Why did you turn him down? You'd be a great Sheriff and you'd live here instead of just visiting. We could see each other all the time, maybe even live together instead of just hooking up when you have time to visit."

Anger flashed along with her words and he enjoyed the show. Feisty and gorgeous and all *his*.

"I don't understand why you said no. I thought you liked it here. With me."

He reached out to touch her. Not quick enough, though, since she was in full fury mode. "Sweet Sherri," he crooned. "Trust me." He crawled across the bed in slow inches, careful to keep her interested in his intent long enough to ensnare. Snagging a hand, he pulled her into the middle of the big bed and settled on top of her. "There, now. This is a better way to discuss this. Will you listen, sweetheart?"

Chin to chin, nose to nose, eye to eye. Close enough to kiss for days, but talk needed to come first. "First, I like my job as it is. I worked damn hard to get a spot with the Rangers. They don't take every applicant and I'm proud of what I do for a living."

Her chin came up. Dammit, her eyes were wet and he hated to see her hurting.

"I didn't know it was such a big deal. Now I understand."

"Good. I want you to understand what you're getting from me." Leaning forward, he pressed as soft kiss on her mouth and then retreated. "While I was in Houston, I talked to several of my bosses. They now agree that the Rangers need a bigger presence in this part of the state. I've been assigned to this region for the next two years, maybe longer."

"Here? In Somewhere?"

Finally, a glimmer of hope turned off the water works and a half smile appeared on that beauty of a face. "Yes. I'm hoping I can find a place to live close by."

Sherri looked around the room before meeting his gaze. "How close were you thinking?"

"I was hoping real close would be an option. What do you think?"

She grinned. "I think that might be arranged. Do you have any references?"

"I think I might have one or two." He rolled over and reached for his pants and she laughed.

"I'm kidding. You don't have to show me your badge or anything, Hart. Come back over here and kiss me. That's all I want right now."

"Yeah, but I want to see what you think about my references. Humor me." Listening to her laugh was like music designed just for his soul. He rolled back toward her and set the square velvet box in front of her.

Her gasp took his breath away. Was that a yes or a no? He was afraid to ask and anxious to hear her answer at the same time.

"What is this?" she whispered.

"Exactly what you think it is. Open it. Please."

Chapter Five
by Jodi Vaughn

"Nothing exciting ever happens in Somewhere." Dr. Candace Roe thoughtfully stirred her crappy cup of hospital coffee and sighed. It was still a few hours into her morning shift in the ER of St. Bethany's, and judging from the non-emergent cases sitting in the waiting room, the day promised to crawl by.

"Are you kidding me? What about that fruit loop that tore off his clothes and decided to go streaking through the college campus?" Shawn Collins offered with enthusiasm. "That's not exactly something you see every day. Although from multiple sources who witnessed the incident said the only thing big on the guy was his mouth. I guess nobody told Mr. Naked he was just embarrassing himself and there was zero possibility of getting some action later from the sorority girls."

"I don't mean that. I mean we never get anything exciting in the ER. All the other hospitals I worked at there was a constant stream of car accidents, stabbings and amputations." She sighed and rested her chin in the palm of her hand. The last excitement this ER saw was a woman going into labor. And even then, the soon to be mother was transported to the Labor and Delivery Unit before Candace could deliver the baby.

Not that it mattered. Babies weren't her thing anyway.

"Well, I heard there might be someone out in triage with the stomach bug. Maybe you'll get lucky and it will turn out to be Ebola." Shawn gave her shoulder a sympathetic squeeze before heading down to check on her patient who'd come in complaining of chest pain.

19

"Rescue 632 to St. Bethany's." The desk speaker phone squawked to life with the incoming ambulance call.

Candace straightened as adrenaline spiked her veins. Reaching over, she pressed the button. "This is St. Bethany's. Go ahead 632." She held her breath and waited to see what kind of report the ambulance was about to relay.

Shawn hurried down the hall and froze besides her listening intently.

"We have a Level One trauma alert, male, late twenties, multiple gunshot wounds to lower abdomen. Patient was unresponsive and in respiratory distress when we arrived on site. Patient is now intubated. We started an IV and are pushing fluids. BP is one-ten over seventy-five, pulse one-thirty, O-two sat is ninety-six percent. Vitals are stable and holding."

"Copy that, 632. We'll be ready for your arrival."

"Not so fast, Dr. Roe. We've also got a second gunshot victim, male, age…" The EMT lowered his voice as he addressed someone else. "Marcus, how old are you?

"None of your damn business. And I'm not a gunshot victim. It's just a scratch." She heard a distinctly male voice in the background, who sounded more pissed off than injured.

"Well, do you have a second gunshot victim or not?" Candace asked, a little confused as to how they got two victims in the same ambulance. Protocol called for one victim per ambulance, unless it was an all-out emergency.

"Make that a second gunshot victim age late twenties. Level Two trauma alert. Gunshot to the left shoulder. Vital signs are stable. He's alert and bleeding is under control. He also said something about being drugged. ETA eight minutes."

"Read you loud and clear, 632, see you when you get here." Candace turned and faced Shawn. who was standing directly behind her listening in on the announcement.

"Looks like things are livening up, Dr. Roe." Shawn narrowed her gaze at her.

She fought back a smile and knew that Shawn was thinking that she'd jinxed them by wishing for some excitement. She wanted to tell the pretty nurse it could be worse. It could be happening at night with a full moon on Friday the thirteenth instead of mid-morning on the Fourth of July.

"You heard the man. Let's' get two rooms set up and ready." Dr. Roe turned and barked out orders to the group of ER nurses that had gathered around her waiting on her instructions. She grabbed the phone and paged the surgeon on call, followed by the hospital supervisor to get the OR ready for surgery.

The staff hurried to get the two rooms set up with anything and everything they might need for the incoming emergencies. Shawn was already on the phone calling up to X-Ray and CT to stand by while Emily prepped the IV fluids with tubing. Mark, the newest RN to the St. Bethany's staff, gathered IV supplies for a secondary IV while the other two available RNs, Phillip and Monica, prepped the bed with pads for the incoming patients.

They might not get a lot of trauma patients but the nurses at St. Bethany's knew their stuff when it came to working as a team to get the job done.

Within a few minutes, the screech of the sirens grew louder. When the ambulance backed up to the ER loading dock, everyone was at their stations and ready to get down to business.

The EMTs rolled the stretcher into the ER bay and locked the wheels before helping to move the gunshot victim to the bed. Following close behind them were Eli Brice in his deputy's uniform, a good looking guy whom she assumed from the conversation in the ambulance was Marcus who had a bloody shoulder, and a woman who looked a lot like that wedding planner wearing a bloodied pink wedding gown.

"I want vital signs, X-ray, CT as well as some blood work for a drug screen. Get a urine sample while you're at it. Let's get a second IV in and hang some Lactated Ringers." She studied the gunshot victim as her nurses recorded and called out the current vital signs, which were stable. She cocked her head as she realized the victim was wearing a bloodied tuxedo that was way too big for him.

She pressed the bell of her stethoscope to the victim's chest to listen to his lungs. They sounded strong with no signs of a hematoma, but a chest X-ray was still in order.

Her cell phone buzzed and she pulled it out of her white coat pocket. After a few brief seconds updating the surgeon she ended the call.

She glanced over at Marcus and nodded toward the patient, then back at the woman in the wedding dress. "Are they supposed to get married?"

"Hell no." Marcus scowled. "He's a psycho."

Touchy subject. She decided to stick to a neutral topic. "What's his name?"

"Murphy Krupp." Marcus's lips pressed into a thin line as he narrowed his eyes.

"How'd he get shot?" She waited for him to answer but his expression didn't change.

"Can't officially say right now. It's an ongoing police investigation." He nodded at Murphy. "Is he going to make it?"

"Right now he's stable. I can't be sure if an organ has been hit or not by the bullet. I just talked to the surgeon and he's not going to wait on the CT scan or X-ray. The OR team is on their way down to get him now. Once the surgeon opens him up he'll know more about internal damage." No sooner were the words out of her mouth than Dr. Jamison came up from behind here.

"Roe, what do we got?" Dr. Jamison was good looking if you considered blond hair, blue eyes and a smile that would make lady parts sing. The female nurses practically swooned every time the surgeon strolled into the room. Good thing Candace was made of sterner stuff.

She handed over the chart she'd been writing on and gave Dr. Jamison the run down on the patient as the anesthesiologist stepped up to the patient to assess him for surgery.

"How did he end up with a bullet in him? Did you shoot him, Marcus?" Jamison quipped.

Marcus didn't reply.

"This is official police business, Jamison. I'm in charge here, so you do your job and I'll do mine." Eli gave the surgeon a smug look and puffed out his chest.

"Whatever, man. Marcus you need to have someone look at that shoulder." Jamison shoved the chart under Murphy's pillow as his OR crew surrounded the bed to begin the transport to surgery.

"Come with me and let's get you in a room so they can get an X-ray of that shoulder." Candace crooked her finger at him and Marcus dutifully followed, with the young woman in tow.

"How about her?" With all the excitement going on, she hadn't noticed how pale the young woman that had come in with the ambulance was. She was trembling and in a wide-eyed trance. Possibly from the shock of witnessing someone get shot. Or maybe she shot him. "Was she hurt too?"

"Tande didn't get shot. Just Murphy." Marcus winced as he sat on the edge of the exam table while Shawn cut away his shirt to assess the damage.

"You must be Tande?" Candace asked, but got no response from the woman. She turned to Marcus. "Does she have any clothes, other than the wedding dress?"

At the word *wedding*, Tande seemed to shake out of whatever silence had been holding her. She looked around and blinked, probably seeing the details of her surroundings for the first time. Candace had seen this type of shock before, too often.

"Is it Saturday?" Her voice shook, then her hands, then her whole body. Marcus tried to move, but Shawn held his shoulder. He looked like he might shake her off as she tried to calm Tande.

"It's Saturday, honey, it'll be okay." Candace spoke calmly.

"But I have the wedding." Tande's voice ratcheted up another level.

"Just let us take a look at this..." She was just about to call for another nurse when Marcus spoke, deep and calming, and Tande's wide eyes focused on him.

"Everything is going to be okay, Tan. I promise. I'll get you to that wedding." He gave her a weak smile.

"I need an X-ray in here, stat." She barked the command at Shawn. She didn't need her patients leaving before they had been properly assessed. Too many things could go wrong.

"X-ray is already here. Let me grab him." Shawn stuck her head out in the hall and a few seconds later the portable machine was being pushed into the room. Everyone stepped outside while the films were taken before going back in.

"It's not bleeding and from what I can see the bullet went clean through." She held up the film to the light. They'd put a rush on the film and had the results up back to her in only a few minutes. "If that's the case and it didn't hit anything, I can clean it up for you down here. You'll need to stay overnight for observation."

"Hell, no. I can't do that." Marcus cut his eyes at Tande and his gaze softened. "I have to get her to that wedding."

Candace frowned at Tande, still not liking the frantic look on her pale face. "Honey, you didn't get shot too did you?"

"No, I'm okay." Her voice shook as she spoke and her face seemed pinched in pain. "But I have got somewhere to be. They'll be expecting me."

"You might not have gotten shot but I don't think you're all right either. You keep nursing your left arm. Did you hurt it?" Dr. Roe waved in the X-ray tech with the portable machine.

"I fell on it when Murphy…when he….It's just aches but it's nothing."

"Doesn't look like nothing to me. It could be dislocated." She turned to Shawn. "Get her in a room. I want to get an X-ray just in case."

"She's not leaving my side." Marcus stood and grimaced as his hand went to cradle his shoulder.

"Fine, fine. Sit back down. I 'll keep both of you in here together." She knew what battles to fight and this wasn't one of them.

"I'll need to talk to Tande, Marcus." Eli stuck his head into the room and addressed the deputy. "I need to get her statement."

"Not now you're not. She's under my care and you can get your statement when I am done." She glared at Eli before shoving him out the door so the tech could get an X-ray.

"Now Dr. Roe, I know you're new in Somewhere, but this is official police business. . ." Eli's face beamed bright red.

"Are you suggesting I put a patient's life in danger and stop medical treatment so you can file some paperwork? Is that what you're telling to me?" Candace crossed her arms over her chest and glared. She'd been in Somewhere long enough to know that there were some men in this town that thought they could run over anyone who wasn't a native. She wasn't having it.

He pressed his lips into a thin line and gave her a curt nod before heading back to the nurse's station to wait.

She put a rush on the X-ray and got the results within minutes. She grabbed the films and walked back into the room where Marcus had pulled Tande onto his lap and was stroking her back with his good hand. She still had that vacant, hysterical look, but at least she wasn't shaking anymore.

"I've got some good news and some bad news." She pulled up a stool and faced the couple.

"Oh, God, what's the bad news?" Tande's face paled. "The bullet hit an artery in Marcus' arm, didn't it?"

Candace snorted. "Actually the bad news is that your arm is dislocated. That's why it hurts so badly. I can fix that here in the ER but it's going to hurt like hell."

"I don't care. I need to get out of here," Tande said. "What about Marcus?"

"The good news is your arm is going to be okay. I can clean it up and you can be discharged, but you're going to have to wear a sling to keep it immobilized while it heals." She gave him a pointed look. She figured he wasn't the type to take orders but she needed him to understand the importance of following the discharge instructions and after care. "If you don't wear it and it won't heal properly and you can face surgery." She put on her best stern face and met Marcus's gaze.

"Fine. Fix us up so we can leave," Marcus said.

"I'll get Shawn in here to begin cleaning your shoulder while I take Tande into another room to get her shoulder worked on. And as soon as I'm done, you can talk to Eli and get his paperwork in order."

"Thanks, Doc. I appreciate it." Marcus gave her a nod before turning his attention back to Tande.

Dr. Roe fought a smile. No wonder Marcus got upset when she suggested Tande was getting married to Murphy. It was clear the cop wanted Tande all to himself.

Chapter Six
by KC Klein

DJ stood over her brother's prone body, thoroughly disgusted with his discombobulated response. His confusion and profound lack of urgency could have something to do with her jolting him from his drunken stupor when she'd started yelling at him.

Derrek squeezed his eyes shut and held up his hands as if to ward off being hit.

As if.

She only resulted to violence at the last resort. Of course, she could always make an exception.

"Wh-what?" Derrek tried again, seemingly still not able to answer her very simple question.

"Where is Brent?" This was the third time she'd asked, not that she was counting or anything. Yeah, she was counting. Actually, she was counting very methodically. It helped control her temper, since this was the second time she'd woken up a stinking drunk man this week alone. *Thank you very much, Chandler Sloan.*

Derrek finally cracked opened his eye lids—pain already evident in his face. She doubted it was over the concern for the whereabouts of his best friend, more likely having to do with the crashing cymbals in his head. "What do you mean? He's not with you?"

"No, he's not." Her voice was super calm, almost scarily so. She wanted to add *you idiot* to the last part, but she refrained. See, who said she didn't have self-control? "Brent's not here. He's not at the hotel. Sally doesn't know where he is, I can't get a hold of Tande, and Brent's not answering his phone. So, I need you to tell me exactly where was the last time you saw him."

That seemed to finally get Derrek's attention. He slowly pushed himself into a sitting position. His hair was a matted mess, his shirt rumpled, and the smell of day old tequila wafting off of him. No wonder Emily had made him sleep out on the couch. DJ would've made him sleep in the barn.

Derrek ran his hands through his hair and tried to focus. "Okay, okay, let's go through this again. Are you sure Brent isn't with you?"

Jesus, she was going to kill him.

Derrek must have caught his imminent death in her eyes, because he quickly tried to pull himself together. "Okay, wait. Let me just think back to last night. I know he was with me at the bar, and then there were some drinks and he was definitely there for that. And then there were some stri..stri...strapping young men who showed up to party with us."

The low simmer of anger that was in her belly turned to a full boil. "*Strapping*. Really, strapping? That's the word you came up with to cover *stripper?*"

Derrek shook his head. "I'm still drunk, that was the best I could do at the moment."

She took deep breath to help find her center, then used really small, and really simple words so he could follow. "And. Then. What. Happened. Derrek?"

His face turned a slight shade of green as he wrapped his arms around his middle. "Um... let me just think. It gets a little foggy after that." He leaned back and closed his eyes. "Just give me a moment...after the toast..."

Derrek's voice drifted off and DJ waited for him to say more. She waited and waited. Until a slight snore escaped from his opened mouth.

That's it.

She turned heel and went into the kitchen. She was back in less than a minute with a large pitcher filled with ice water.

There were only a few times in her life where she could pinpoint with absolute satisfaction at how karma worked. This was one of them.

DJ upended the pitcher on top of her brother's head. A high-pitched, very girly-like scream was followed by a long string of words their mama would've washed his mouth out for using.

She smiled after every one of them.

"What the hell, DJ?" Derrek was on his feet and looking madder than a two headed snake, cold and soaking wet. "I'm going to kill you!"

Derrek took a step toward her and DJ took off running around the couch.

"Where's Brent?" she screamed, doing her best to keep furniture between her and her enraged brother. Maybe this time he'd answer the question.

He stopped chasing her and held his head. "What do you mean? He's not with you?"

Holy, Mother of—

Just then, a cell phone rang, cutting off DJ's thought. They both glanced down at Derrek's phone, that had been left lying on the couch. The name "Brent" came up on the caller ID. They looked at each other. Then back down at the phone.

Both dived head first into the couch.

They hadn't wrestled since they were kids. It hadn't been a fair fight back then, but even so DJ had learned a few moves and gotten some cheap shots in now and again. If it hadn't been a fair before, it sure had evened out now. Derrek may have been a hundred pounds heavier and a lot stronger, but he was slowed down by a night of drinking while DJ was fueled up by a night of worry.

He made it on top of the couch first, but DJ was able to unbalance him by using his momentum and pushing him to the floor. Derrek had the phone in his grasp, but not good enough, since DJ ripped the phone out of his grip. She turned to run when Derrek pulled a Hail Mary and caught her foot. She went down, barely catching herself before smacking face first.

Derrek quickly sat on her back, pinning her to the floor like a bug. She tucked the phone closer to her stomach not willing to give up yet.

"Let me up!" she screamed, barely able to take in air. He was a lot heavier than when they'd done this before.

"Say uncle," he said, bouncing up and down. "And that you're sorry about the water."

"I'm telling!" DJ yelled trying to get her foot up to kick him in the ribs.

"What in God's name is going on?"

They both looked up and saw Emily standing in front of them, hands on her hips, her no-nonsense nurse tone on full volume.

"She took my phone," Derrek said.

"He wouldn't let me answer it," DJ whined.

"It's my phone!"

"He's my fiancé!"

"Enough, both of you!" Emily cut in and stretched out her hand. "Give me the phone. I'll answer it."

But it was too late. The phone had gone silent.

Brent stared down at his cell phone with his mouth open. It had taken him all morning of waiting until Wally left so he could ask the other, baby-faced deputy for his phone call, and now that he'd finally gotten it, Derrek wasn't answering his freaking *phone!*

The wide-eyed deputy looked at Brent with a bit of awe and some star-struck thrown in for good measure. Brent pressed his advantage. He glanced down at the young man's name tag. "It's Rankins, right? My phone got disconnected, Deputy Rankins. The phone service here is unpredictable. Let me try again."

He didn't even wait for permission, just ended the call and dialed. *Come on, Derrek. Come on!*

"Hello!"

Brent recognized the voice on the other end immediately, and his heart sank. "Hey babe, how's it going?"

Did he sound cheerful enough? Confident and not at all like a man calling for a bail out of jail?

"Where are you? Are you okay? Are you hurt?" DJ's questions came like rapid fire. *Oh hell, she's had her coffee.*

"What? No. Everything's just fine. But… um… I was hoping you could put Derrek on the phone. Is he there?"

There was some drawn out silence that made Brent think about hot flashes again until DJ finally spoke.

"Derrek is right here, but he told me he didn't know where you were. So where exactly are you? This doesn't have anything to do with those threats, does it? You told me there was nothing to worry about. Oh my God, Brent, are you in danger?"

Dammit, the threats. Of course, DJ would be scared out of her mind. "No, babe, I'm fine, just fine. I'm totally safe. It's almost like I have thick metal bars between me and anyone who might want to hurt me." He laughed at his own joke.

There was a second pause in the conversation. He started to dread these silences more than the actual conversation.

"What's going on, Brent?" Her voice changed. Concern and fear were quickly swallowed up by anger.

He sighed. "I'm in jail. Tell Derrek to get a hold of Sally so she can get me some bail money."

"Jail? Bail money? Exactly how much money are we talking?"

"According to Wally, upward of a hundred thousand dollars."

"Holy—"

"Yep."

Brent finished his conversation with a few "I love you's" that weren't reciprocated, and then handed his phone back to Rankins. The boy-man deputy gave him a small smile.

"Thanks," Brent said as the young deputy started to escort him back to the holding cell. Deputy Rankins' walk slowed to a crawl as he fidgeted at Brent's side.

"Is there something on your mind, Deputy? If so just ask?'

"It's Tyler. Call me Tyler." He cleared his throat. "Are you Brent Kane? The singer who wrote the song *Love Walks In*?"

"That's what they tell me."

"I'm a big fan. A really big fan and I'm so sorry this whole thing has happened. I hope your people get you out of this real quick."

Brent sensed a kindred spirit and wasn't above using his celebrity status to gain a few favors. "There is something that you can do for me. Can you go and tell Deputy Young or Deputy Brice that I would like to see them."

The boy scrunched up his face in hesitation. "I would. I really would, but Deputy Brice is on a call, and Deputy Young is out sick, sounded like a bad hangover if you ask me."

Brent knew all about the bad hangover that Deputy Jeff Young had. He'd like to add to it by punching him in the face. "Would it be a lot of trouble to maybe call him? He's a real good friend of mine and I think he'd want to know that I'm locked up down here."

Brent had started to put two and two together from last night and he wouldn't put it past Eli and Jeff to play some kind of practical joke on him. Wally was just the sort of idiot who would fall for it.

"Um, yeah, um sure, but he' specifically told me never to call him at home unless it's an emergency."

There was a laundry list of things that wanted to tumble from Brent's mouth—the ruining of his public image, the paparazzi getting a hold of this story, and him missing his own wedding. Instead, he just nodded. "Yeah, this is an emergency."

Tyler finished escorting him back to the cell and hurried off, Brent hoped, in order to call Jeff. Now, all he had to do was wait and pray that this whole thing would be straightened out before DJ got here.

Brent woke up to the sound of a lock on his cell turning. Deputy Young was opening the door, his face already contrite with an apology. "Oh God, Brent, I am so sorry. I mean, I can't believe that this really happened. I had no idea Wally would take it this far."

Jeff looked as bad as Brent felt. Day old scruff covered his face and neck, stained jeans thrown on under what looked like the shirt he'd slept in. A slicked back mess on top of his head that hadn't seen hide nor hair of shampoo. Yeah, it looked like Jeff had showered about as recently as Brent had.

"What the hell, Jeff? What happened?" Brent followed the tall, husky deputy out of the cell. He did a quick turn and waved to Randall who systematically gave him the bird.

Jackass.

"It was a prank on Wally," Jeff said. "I didn't really think he'd act on it, and if he did, he'd realize pretty quick what had happened. But I don't think that guy's playing with a full deck. There's something wrong with him."

"Yah think? Dammit, Jeff, I almost missed my wedding. Do you know how pissed DJ would've been?"

"Um, that's another thing." Jeff ran his hand through his unwashed hair and shifted his weight from foot to foot. "Yeah, DJ is here."

"Already?" It wasn't as if Brent didn't know she was on her way, he'd just hoped he could've had all this cleared up before she'd gotten here.

"Yeah, she's here, and um, she is very pissed. I don't think I've ever heard a woman scare a man so efficiently that Tyler was tripping over himself trying to get behind Edna's reception desk and out of the line of fire."

Brent smiled. *That's my girl.* "Where is she?"

"Up front. We were too afraid to let her back, in case she decided to get hostile."

Brent tried to hide his laugh behind his hand, but didn't quite succeed.

"This is no laughing matter, Brent. Geez, it was just a joke. You understand right, bro?"

Jeff had just let him spend a whole night in a holding cell, but oh, they were bros now. *Jerk.* "Yeah, I understand."

"Do you think you could ask DJ if she'd be willing not say anything? The whole department is shook up over Randall being in jail, and I'm pretty sure everyone is going to be investigated. I really would hate for Eli and I to lose our jobs over this."

Brent turned the corner and could see his girl pacing in the few feet of unoccupied space in the already crowded reception area. She had on her normal outfit of shorts, tank top, and a cowboy hat. He didn't think he'd ever been so happy to see her in his life. Hell, maybe they should just elope. He'd take her just like that and run to Vegas right now.

"Brent? Brent, did you hear me?" Jeff was still talking.

"Jeff, just be glad that you got here in time for me to make my wedding. If not, Jesus himself couldn't have saved your job." Brent pushed passed, leaving Jeff alone to figure out if Brent was serious or not. Oh, he was serious.

He walked out to DJ. "I'm here, baby."

DJ whipped around, fire in her eyes, stance battle ready. "What the hell, Brent? I can't believe you did this. I can't believe…" Her voice broke. "I can't believe… I was worried about you."

Brent wrapped his arms around her and cradled her against his shoulder. DJ wasn't scared of much, but losing the people she loved did it to her every time. "It's okay. Everything's all right. I'm here now."

He felt her sigh against his chest and relax slightly. "Do you think it's bad luck for the groom to see his bride before the wedding?"

Brent started to laugh, and then DJ joined in until both of them were holding each other up.

"I think we can safely say that things couldn't possibly get any worse from this point on," Brent said.

DJ wiped at her eyes. "Don't say that. That is such bad luck."

He shrugged "Come on, what else could happen? The only thing left to go wrong is if your wedding dress goes missing or the reception gets set on fire."

Oh wait, that already happened. He'd confess it after some coffee. Or next week, or maybe never, if he could keep her from finding out.

DJ gasped and slapped his arm. "Stop, don't even say that. No, thank God, that's the one thing I can say for sure, my wedding dress and your tux are safe. I gave them to Murphy for safe keeping. At least that's one thing we don't have to worry about."

Brent picked her up and crushed her in a bear hug. "See, perfect. It's all going to be great, but even if it's not, I'd still marry you wearing exactly what you have on."

She laughed. "Yeah, you can say that because I've actually showered. You on the other hand… I have ranch hands that smell better than you."

"What?" Brent pulled back in mock horror. "Which ranch hands have you been sniffing around? I'll have them thrown off my ranch—" he snapped his fingers "just like that."

DJ pulled back to look him in the eye. "*Your* ranch?"

He couldn't resist. That's what he did best—make her laugh. "Oh, sorry, *the* ranch."

"You're pushing it, Rock Star."

Brent scratched his head and threw her a completely confused look. *"Derrek's* ranch?"

She socked him in the arm… hard. "I swear, I'm so close to leaving you here. You know, maybe my ranch hand wasn't so bad after all. He did fill out a pair of jeans really well."

"Okay, okay," he said, putting his arm around her shoulders and walking toward the door. "We're going to have the best wedding ever!"

"You promise?"

"I promise. Hey," he said, looking down at her, loving the feel of her tucked under his arm. "Have I ever let you down?"

Her annoyed look had always been his favorite.

"Okay, besides that one time."

She snorted.

"Oh and that other time, also. What I meant to say was from here on out I'll never let you down."

"I'm counting on it." DJ tilted her chin up, her eyes bright and her mouth in a wide smile.

And more than anything in the world, Brent wanted to keep that smile on DJ's face because one thing he knew for sure—when she reached her limit there'd be no going back.

He just had to make sure that the rest of this day went off without a hitch, because hand to God, one more thing went wrong and he'd be put in jail for real—this time for killing Tande and Claire.

Chapter Seven
by RL Syme

Sitting at the breakfast table, at eleven a.m. on the day of a big client's wedding felt so indulgent. Claire picked at the remains of the omelet Aidan had made her and sipped her mimosa. Another indulgence.

She downed the rest of the breakfast cocktail and turned the notebook beside her plate to look at her to-do list.

1. *Check in with Murphy.*
2. *Check in with Tande.*
3. *Get Derrek the rings.*

Claire Milton-Conley
Claire Conley
Claire M. Conley

Somehow, her to-do list had taken a left turn when she wrote the word *rings*. Every time she thought about DJ and Brent's rings, she thought of her own. Her new ring—the one Aidan had given her last week. And then, she couldn't stop thinking about her wedding, and about being Aidan's wife.

Her whole stomach did a nosedive. *Aidan's wife.*

She pushed the plate away and dragged the notebook fully in front of her, across the knobby oak table Aidan had made for his house. The paper crinkled under her hand as she ripped the top sheet away, balled it up, and tossed it toward the garbage can.

Aidan's laugh made her free-falling stomach find purchase and land.

Her smile was immediate and easy. "Don't make fun of my throwing, Aid."

He picked up the crumpled paper and tossed it into the garbage can. They both made crowd noises and raised their hands in the air at the same time. It was a silly ritual, but it was theirs.

"It was an assist, right?" Aidan's smile mirrored hers and he slipped his arms around her waist, kissing her neck.

"It was an assist." Her hand instinctively went to the back of his head, threading through his hair as she held him to her.

He bit the soft flesh on the side of her neck and held her tighter.

"I can't right now, Aid."

His hands moved higher. "Why not? You don't have to be to the ranch until noon, and you know how I—" his voice dipped lower "to relax you…"

She let the tiny thrills soar through her for just a moment longer. He did relax her. But the mood she was in that morning, she wouldn't have been able to stop with a quickie, even though that was all she had time for. "I need to jump in the shower and get ready to head out to the ranch," she said.

Aidan growled into her neck. "Perfect."

Claire laughed. "No, Aid. I mean it. Nothing you are doing is going to lead to me getting out of this house on time."

"I just want to make love to my future wife."

She closed her eyes and leaned her head back into his shoulder. She loved hearing him say that. But the blank piece of paper caught her eye and she shook her head. "We'll have plenty of time for that after the wedding."

Aidan groaned and slid into the chair beside her, keeping one hand on her leg and kneading her thigh. "I just want to enjoy having you here while you're here."

Claire picked up the pen and rewrote the first three items on her to-do list. She couldn't help laughing when the word *rings* made her think about her name again. The name discussion had been a long one, that had lasted most of the week, and neither of them could come to a firm decision. It was one of a thousand conversations they were going to have to have before they started planning their own wedding.

"It won't be long," she said. "I promise, I'm going to find a way to get back here for good."

"Did you talk to Tande?"

She swallowed against her suddenly dry throat. "I talked to her yesterday, a couple of times."

"And?" Aidan picked up one of the blueberries that still sat on her plate and popped it into his mouth.

"It could have gone better."

"Do you still think it was a good idea to wait to tell her?"

Claire shrugged. "I guess we'll never know if it would've been better. I could have handled it better, I'm sure."

Aidan ate another blueberry. "Is it time?"

She glanced at the clock. "Y'know, it's funny, I didn't even notice that you'd hidden it until just now."

He reached into the pocket of his jeans. "I could wait until after you shower."

"No, I guess I'd better have it now. It would be good to check in with both Murphy and Tande and make sure we're all ready to go."

Claire held out her hand,

Aidan produced her cell phone. "I really maybe should wait until after you shower," he said.

"Give it." She grabbed the phone, smiling to herself. He'd taken it away from her the previous night after Tande had left the rehearsal dinner and Marcus skulked off to lick his wounds. Claire sighed.

"That sounded like a weight-of-the-world moment, Claire. Are you sure you want that phone back?" Aidan kept his fingers around the edge of the cell and tugged on it just enough to make her stop and think.

Did she really want the phone? No. She wanted this wedding to be over, God help her. It was just too much drama for her taste.

"I was just thinking I should've called Tande last night."

Aidan pulled the phone out of her hand. "You made the right choice. Tande is having a hard week. She needed to cool off."

Claire reached toward him. "I know, but I should call her now."

"You're not going to be able to help her with Marc. You've got to let that one go, babe." Aidan held the phone over his shoulder, out of her arms-length.

"I don't want to help her with Marcus. I want to help her get over him."

He grabbed her champagne flute and headed for the kitchen, still hanging on to her phone. "I told you, I've got someone in mind for Marcus. We'll set him up with a couple of girls and he'll be good."

Claire twirled the pen and listened to Aidan refill her mimosa. She added a fourth item to her to-do list.

4. Find Marcus another girlfriend

"It feels so strange to think about separating the two of them," Claire said.

"It'll be better for them both."

She remembered the look on Marcus's face when he saw Tande in that coral dress she'd worn the previous day. She saw that look all the time, when Aidan was caught off-guard by something and just looked at her with that brazen, raw desire in his eyes. "Poor Marcus."

Aidan put the mimosa on the table and slipped the phone down next to her notebook. He pressed his lips into hers for a long, luxurious moment. She ran her tongue along the edge of his lip and he grabbed the sides of her face, going deeper, harder, longer.

Claire made herself pull away with a smile. "You're covert, mister."

He stayed close and chuckled to himself. "A guy's gotta try." He kissed her forehead. "I need to finish staining that chair before we leave. Are you gonna shower?"

She picked up the phone and powered it up. "I will. Just let me check my messages."

"You do that. I'll be in the back."

Claire grabbed his hand as he walked away. For a long moment, she just stared at him, his same old fire and rescue t-shirt, his faded jeans, his slightly mussed, dark hair hanging over his left eye again.

This man was going to be her husband.

She stood and went to her tiptoes to kiss him. Hard. "I love you, y'know?"

"I know." He smacked her butt and left the room. From the hallway, he yelled back, "Don't forget, we have to head to the ranch in an hour. So go think of how much you love me in the shower."

Claire couldn't help the laugh that bubbled out of her. She sat at the notebook, trying to remember if there was anything else she was supposed to do before they got to the ranch. It was tempting to start writing out her name over and over, but the time was advancing quickly enough that she should leave even the to-do list and get ready for the big day.

It was going to be a long one.

She pressed a button on the bottom of her phone and boxes popped up, as she'd expected. Someone would have left a message, even if it was just Tande calling to say she was…

Hold on a second.

Claire pressed the button again.

Voicemail and message from Saddles for Hope Ranch. Seven. *SEVEN?*

"Hi, uh, Claire Milton? This is the number that's on the emergency contact for the Diaz-Kane wedding. I, uh, I guess this is an emergency. I see there's another name on here. A Tande Walker, too. I'll call her. Uh, bye."

Claire's pulse steadily raced through the entire call and by the time she clicked on the next message, her breath was coming faster.

"Hi, Claire Milton? This is Michael at Saddles for Hope Ranch. Yeah, I tried the other emergency number for the Diaz-Kane wedding and she's not answering either. I need you to call me back as soon as you can. We have a bit of a situation here."

In the background of the message, Tande could hear another male voice adding some words to the message, but she couldn't make them out. Instead of trying to play Phone Operator, she just went to the next message.

"Claire, this is Michael again at the ranch. Jeremy thinks I should just tell you what happened so you can get the message and tell us what to do."

Claire took a deep breath and steeled herself. Seven messages before eleven in the morning. Something was really wrong.

The message continued, detailing something about a fire the previous night taking down the hay wall, or something. Claire's heart was skipping beats and falling in on itself. She was surprised she wasn't actually having a heart attack.

"So, just call us back and tell us what you want us to do. Thanks, bye."

The voicemail ended. Claire looked at the other four little blue dots and almost couldn't bring herself to click on the next one.

"Hi, Claire. I still can't get ahold of Tande Walker and we don't want to bother DJ or Brent about this. I just need to know what to do with this big hole in the hay wall. Jeremy and I finally got the parking lot cleaned up and we need to know what to do with the rest of the hay wall. Call me back when you get a chance."

She finally had to set the phone down on the table. She wasn't sure she had the mental fortitude to listen to any more. Why had she ever let Aidan convince her to shut her phone off?

Claire clicked over to the text messages. Nothing. No calls or texts from Tande. Or from Murphy.

What the actual hell was going on?

She called Tande first. Straight to voicemail. Then Murphy. Also voicemail. What the hell? Had everyone taken the night off? Who was minding the freaking business if everyone was off having a lark?

Claire tried to remember the night before, but with very little luck. She'd seen Tande leave, followed by Marcus, out the side door, and tried not to think about it when Aidan pointed out that she was biting her fingernails again.

But those two. Really. They were like gasoline and fire. It didn't take long for everything to explode.

Marcus had come back inside for a bit, but Claire didn't remember seeing Tande again, and when Marcus had wrestled Rhonda's brother away from his mission to terrorize Adam VonBrandt—which, really, God bless the man for saving an idiot from a beatdown—she hadn't seen him come back.

Had they gone somewhere together?

Had they slept together?

Claire pressed Tande's name again on her call list. Still, straight to voicemail. And Murphy was still the same. She texted Murphy.

Call me. Right now.

And the same to Tande. If her phone was off, she wouldn't get it. But what could she do? Call Marcus?

In short order, she'd found him in her contacts list and called him. His phone, at least, rang. And rang. And rang. When the line went live, the noise in the background was so loud, Claire almost couldn't hear the voice.

"Marcus?" she found herself yelling, trying to be heard over the noise.

"Is this Claire Milton?" a female voice responded. Not Tande.

"It is."

"Your name comes up on this phone as Claire Milton, so I just wanted to make sure. I found it in the parking lot at the River Hotel and was just about to take it to the front desk. Do you know whose phone this is?"

Claire bit her knuckle. Marcus's phone in the lot at the River Hotel? Tande not answering? Had they gone back to Tande's room?

A little squeal made its way out of Claire's mouth.

"Are you okay?" the woman asked.

"I'm fine. Sorry. Just looking for a friend." Claire pressed the end button on her screen and chewed at the knuckle.

She was going to kill Tande. She would actually murder her. The ranch was calling frantically, Murphy was AWOL, and Tande had shacked up with her ex all night in some hotel room?

Claire put the phone down and tried to center her thoughts. Her heart in her throat, she let out a long breath.

DJ. She had to call DJ and, as calmly as possible, make sure everything was going all right with the girls. They should have been on their way to the salon for their hair and makeup appointments, and she didn't want to worry them. But given the general luck everyone seemed to have at this wedding, better safe than sorry.

Chapter Eight
by Becca Boyd

Eli Brice collected the folders from the front seat of his cruiser and walked in to the station through the back door. It seemed quiet uptown, even though the hospital had been a madhouse.

He had to admit, that Dr. Roe had a great ass. He hadn't even minded the paperwork Marcus's girlfriend had generated, because it meant a few more minutes talking to a pretty doctor. Maybe she was single. His sister was on him to start dating again, maybe Candace Roe was into small town deputies.

Doubtful.

The last two days had been eventful enough, he hadn't had time to think about anything but work. Filing Marcus and Tande's statements would give him a chance to close out what might otherwise have been a quiet shift. Only an hour left.

As soon as he opened the door into the main office, he could tell something was off. Two women were yelling off to the side, near the holding cells. A big group of people milled around in the front office, in reception. Jeff and Wally huddled off near one of the desks, engaged in some kind of deep conversation, and near them, Brent Kane picked up a girl in a cowboy hat and swung her around.

Thankfully, said girl turned out to be his fiancée, or Eli might have had to throw him back in his cell.

Eli placed the folders on his desk and eyed Wally. "What happened here?"

"I'm handling it," Wally said.

"We're handling it," said Jeff.

Neither of them appeared to be actually handling anything. Wally looked annoyed and smug, which meant he was likely to get a beat-down from one of the senior deputies. Jeff smelled like slop-time at Elmer Winkle's pig farm and could have given Homeless Jim a run for his unwashed money.

Eli walked toward the mini-mob, trying to decide if he needed to break up the scene or not.

They kept talking in small groups, ignoring him. One little circle was bunch of off-duty deputies, and the other consisted of a couple of city commissioners, and the right honorable JJ Walker—former owner of Everyday Joe's.

Wally and Jeff just kept whispering.

"Hey, DJ!" Eli called after her as she and her fiancé headed for the door. She turned around and gave him a pained smile.

"Eli."

Her fiancé, country rock star extraordinaire, Brent Kane, gave Eli a disgusted look. "You'd better not be trying to arrest me again. Whatever it is, I didn't do it."

Eli held out his hands. "I'm sorry about this, Brent. I know it got out of hand last night. I figured Wally would have released you by now."

Brent grunted. "If he'd had his way, I would be in maximum security by now."

"I really thought he would have released you a long time ago."

"Yeah, well, he didn't."

Eli took in a deep breath and held it. "I'm sorry this got out of hand. I hope it didn't cause any inconvenience."

"Other than almost missing my wedding, I'm totally fine." Brent's sneer was only half-hearted when DJ put her hand on his chest.

"Speaking of weddings," she said. "We've already missed our appointments at the salon, so Emily's calling Claire and Tande to get them to bring the stylists out to the ranch and meet us there. And we've got to get some breakfast, or lunch, I guess. I am starving."

Brent looked down at her and didn't speak for several heartbeats. When he did finally break eye contact with her, his spirits were much brighter. He laughed and offered his hand to Eli. "No hard feelings, right?"

Eli returned the handshake. "Honestly, if I'd have been here instead of out on a call this morning, and I'd seen you in holding, I would've made Wally release you, no matter what he thought."

"A prank too far." Brent's voice was more serious than it had been the previous night at his bachelor party when they were all joking around at Everyday Joe's about strippers and pranks and arresting people.

"I didn't even know they'd taken you in."

"Water. Bridge." Brent made a gesture with one hand under the other and plastered on a smile. "And all that."

"Well, I'm glad they got you processed and out. I'm sure Wally hadn't even filed the paperwork yet, so it won't show up as an arrest or anything."

DJ pushed her hat forward. "Let's just hope the paparazzi aren't camped outside waiting to get a shot of you."

Eli thumbed behind him. "I came in the back and it was quiet."

DJ shrugged. "There weren't any out front when I came in, so it's possible they don't even know you're here."

Brent took her hand and pulled her back through the office. "Better safe than sorry, though." His steps were a little too quick. Maybe he knew something Eli didn't know. Or, more likely, something DJ didn't know.

A woman's voice called out in sharp tones. "We love you, Brent!"

Another echoed. "Yes, Brent! We love you!"

Brent's shoulders went up around his ears as DJ said, "What in the damn hell is all that?"

The poor cowboy rock star slunk through the back door saying to his bride, "I'll tell you all about it once I get some coffee."

There were some moments that Eli didn't regret being single. This was one of them. God help him if he ever had *that* look in his eye. The one Brent had, where you just knew he was fixing to make a fool of himself over some girl.

Nope. Eli might be willing to admire a hot-ass doctor, but he was not interested in going googly-eyed over anybody. Not now, not ever. No matter what his sister told him.

He fixed his sights on Wally. The rookie deputy thing would only carry so far with the Sheriff. Although, given what he'd heard at the coffee shop that morning, the Sheriff wasn't even the Sheriff anymore.

Might have been why the commissioners were all huddled behind Edna's desk. Could be, they'd make Allan the new Sheriff, then the discipline over the pranks would commence. Allan was a no-shit-taker if ever there was one.

Wally sidled up to Eli and went with the preemptive strike. "I let him go."

Jeff smirked. "You did."

"You never should have arrested him in the first place, Wally."

"But y'all said…" The rookie stopped, looking around the room for someone to back him up.

"It's called hazing, rook." Jeff clapped him on the back. "Puts hair on your chest."

Eli shook his head. "Even if another deputy tells you he knows someone is guilty of something, you still always have to look at the evidence."

Wally's mouth wagged, wordlessly.

"No matter what. Even if it was Randall. We still have to have probable cause to arrest someone for a crime." Eli put his finger down on top of the pile of paperwork on Jeff's desk. "There always has to be evidence."

"But…" Wally kept looking for sympathy, but Eli had reached his limit.

"We shouldn't have been pranking you about something like arresting a guy the night before his wedding." Eli walked to his desk and picked up his own paperwork. "Especially given where I've been all morning."

"How's Marcus?" Wally followed and Jeff wasn't far behind.

"He's fine, as always." Eli opened the file and pulled out Marcus's statement. "He turned in his badge and gun until the investigation is over."

Jeff took the piece of paper and looked it over. "Whoa."

Eli nodded. "Yeah."

Wally reached for it, but Jeff kept reading and turned his body to shield the statement.

"Whoa-oh," Jeff repeated, slower, drawlier.

Eli laughed. "Yeah. I know."

"Did you arrest the Krupp kid?" Jeff handed the statement back and Eli slipped it into the folder before Wally could get his hands on it.

"He's in surgery, but Gibson stayed at the hospital."

Jeff swept the room in a wide gesture. "Not that we'd have any room in holding, even if you brought him in."

Eli nodded. The group of men still engaged in deep conversation in the front seemed to have grown. The clump of deputies had joined the commissioners. Allan VonBrandt, Greg Lipton, and Alex Landry had seniority in the Long Rock County Sheriff's Department, and would have had the most to lose if the court started indicting more people than just Randall in connection with this city hall case.

He wasn't much for politics, especially when it came to his job, but he knew enough to guess that tensions were high already, without fires and shootings and such.

With Randall arrested, they'd likely appoint an interim sheriff, and those three guys were the most likely candidates. Eli didn't want anything to do with any of it. He just wanted to put his head down and get off work in an hour so he could head back out to the lake and get in some fishing.

Maybe think a little more about Dr. Roe and her fine ass.

Or not.

"Who comes on at noon?" Eli wondered, trying to ignore the drama at the front of the office.

"It was supposed to be Johnson and Gibson, but with Gibby at the hospital still, I might stay through," Jeff said. "I could use the overtime."

"Aren't you supposed to be off-shift?" Eli said to Wally, who had the dumbest, wide-eyed look on his face.

They needed to start being nicer to Wally. He wasn't going to be the rookie for much longer and he wasn't a half-bad guy. Just a little on the dumb side at times.

Like when he buddies told him they knew where Jimmy Hoffa was buried, or that an LA celebrity in town for a wedding was really running a prostitution ring out of Houston. Not the brightest candle.

Wally mumbled something about staying to take down the kingpin and both Jeff and Eli let loose laughter that stopped the conversation across the room.

Eli nodded at JJ Walker and picked up his file again, pretending not to notice the presence of the other men in the room at all.

"What's going on up there?" Wally nodded. "They get awful quiet when I come over to the desk."

Eli waved his hand. "Ah, let them be. They're trying to deal with this Randall stuff. We've got other fish to fry." He handed the folders to Wally. "Write up the sheet for Murphy Krupp and take it down to Gibby at the hospital. And then go off shift, for shit's sake. You need a shower like nobody's business."

Wally shrugged. "I can stay for a bit still."

"Nah, Brice is right." Jeff pushed at the rookie. "You've been here all night, you should get on home."

The kicked-puppy-dog look on Wally's face made Eli stop. They'd been mean enough to the poor guy for a while. "I'll tell you what, if you promise not to talk, you can come out to the lake with me when I'm off-shift."

Wally opened his mouth to comment, but thought better. Instead, he scurried over to his desk and pulled out some paperwork.

Eli chuckled. "Poor guy. We need to take it easy on him for a while."

Jeff flicked at something on Eli's desk. "I think I talked Brent out of suing the department, at least."

"Yeah, that could have been a nightmare. But he has bigger fish to fry."

"Meaning?"

"Meaning, between the fire out at the ranch and the shooting at the hotel, his weekend is a shambles. His bride is on edge, and we just arrested some of his fans for trying to stop his wedding."

Jeff's thick eyebrows rounded. "And his wedding planner shot her assistant, who shot one of our deputies."

"Right." Eli leaned back in his chair. "When things go wrong on this level, the last thing Brent's going to be thinking about is suing the Sheriff. Not when he'll be lucky to get married today. Or at all."

Chapter Nine
by Emma Roman

Fourth of July.

Wedding day at the ranch.

Anna Granger was grateful for the money the Kane-Diaz wedding was bringing in, but it was like slapping a miniature Band-Aid on a gushing artery wound. It took thousands of dollars every month to keep this place going. Even a huge donation of hay only helped so much.

She strolled down the long gravely driveway that led from her cabin on the Saddles For Hope property to the main entrance road. Her booted toe caught on a larger rock and she kicked it to the side, enjoying the clattering sound it made as it skittered over into the grass. She loved living on the ranch instead of in town. Plus it was cheaper. The cabin might not be much, but she wouldn't want to be anywhere else. No nosy neighbors. No ambient noise –just a peaceful existence with the occasional howl of wild animals at night.

Right now that peaceful life was crashing around her –a fiery storm from the heavens. Bills were mounting since her main investor passed away almost a year ago, right before donation time. The wealthy Houston benefactor hadn't left *any* endowment for SFH after supporting eighty percent of her budget since opening two years ago. If it hadn't been for the surprisingly large donation made by Shawn Collins, a local and recent divorcé, earlier this year, she would've had to close down months ago. As it was, she had enough to last a couple more months before she would have to start laying off staff.

But, today was a wedding day and Independence Day. Just for today she would set aside her worry and stress. She took a deep breath of the piney morning air and stopped, scrunching her eyebrows.

A sedan was stopped on the side of her driveway, just hidden from view of the main road by a line of trees. And it was moving. Well…it was rocking in place.

"Oh, geeez." College kids were all over this town, but she'd never seen any pull onto the ranch property before and park! And…God, were they actually…?

A hand palmed the glass from inside the backseat, reminiscent of an iconic movie scene involving a sinking ship. They were going to be sinking soon, if they didn't get their naked asses dressed and off her property.

"Hey!" she shouted, continuing to approach the rocking sedan. Gritting her teeth, she covered her eyes with one hand and reached for the back door handle with her other. She'd scare these kids straight and it would be the last time they ever tried to use her driveway as their personal make-out parking spot.

"You two should be ashamed of yourselves!" she barked as two half naked bodies tumbled out of the back seat of the sedan onto the grass beside the driveway. "This is a public ranch. Children come here!"

The guy yanked his pants back up in a jiffy, but damn he'd had a nice ass and he was bigger than the average college kid.

"How dare you use my driveway to…" Anna stopped, catching a clearer view of the barely-clothed woman. Blonde. Small. Very familiar.

Good God! It was one of the wedding planners! Not a couple of horny college kids. This was…

"Claire?"

A mortified screech tore from the wedding planner's throat as she frantically shoved her skirt and blouse back into place. Anna swallowed a chuckle and turned away as the blonde and her *significant other* scrambled to completely re-clothe themselves.

"You know they have these really nifty places called bedrooms for the sort of frolicking y'all were enjoying. Why on earth would you *choose* to try and do that in the back seat of that cramped little car?"

"I'm so sorry, Anna. I-It-" Claire stuttered.

"Aidan Conley," he said, extending his hand. "Sorry to be trouble, Ms. Granger. I've been trying to convince her all day that she needed to relax." He shrugged his broad shoulders and rolled his head, popping a few vertebrae. "And she finally agreed with me," he finished, winking at her. "Couldn't let the moment pass."

Anna met his mischievous gaze and shook her head, a grin spreading across her face. "I'll shake your hand another time, hon. But, it's nice to meet you."

He gave her a sheepish grin and shoved his hand back in his pocket.

That man was a handful and a half. Why couldn't she find a guy who would make love to her in the back of a car because he just couldn't wait to be with her?

"Well, since you're both decent now, I suppose we should all continue toward the barn and see what needs to still be done to get this wedding up and running."

A cheerful ring tone beeped from the back seat and Claire dove for the phone. She swiped the screen, her lips moving as she read the text message.

Anna stood with Aidan as the wedding planner's face turned ashen.

"Claire?" Aidan said, his tone asking the question.

"They didn't have time to go to the salon. Something about a prank and bailing Brent out of jail. What are we going to do?" Claire's tone rose with each word. "I still can't find Tande and now the girls have no hair appointments."

The cell phone in her had beeped again. "You've got to be kidding me," Claire muttered under her breath.

"What?" Aidan reached out and touched Claire's arm. "What's wrong?"

"The dresses," Claire squeaked, pointing to the back seat. "She says they're in our car."

Aidan stepped forward and bent over, reaching into the sedan. He came back with a handful of black crinkled dress bags.

A burst of laughter exploded from Anna, echoing through the treetops around them. "You guys defiled the bridesmaids dresses. Horny college students everywhere would be proud."

The guy looked like he wanted to laugh, but thought better of it and refrained, pressing his lips so tightly together that they lost blood flow and turned white.

"Ohhhhhh," Claire said, though it was more of a screech than a recognizable word.

"Oh, they'll be fine," Anna said. "I'll see you up at the arena."

"You don't want a ride?" Aidan asked, gesturing the back seat of the car with that same damn twinkle in his eye.

"You're incorrigible," she said, shaking her head. "I'll pass, thanks."

He chuckled and herded the still muttering Claire into the sedan, before he slid into the drivers' seat and chucked the bridesmaids dresses over his shoulder into the back seat.

Another squawk from Claire made Anna snort with laughter again. They backed onto the main road and then turned forward toward the main buildings.

Anna waited a moment for the gravel and dust to settle before continuing on her stroll. As she passed the hay wall, she stopped and stared for a few seconds. It looked different, but she couldn't put her finger on it.

Jeremy and Michael were out in one of the exercise pens with Lucky and Widget. Both waved as she passed and she lifted her hand, returning the greeting.

Both boys looked guilty as sin, but she didn't have time to ask what they were hiding from her at the moment. And if it was anything really bad, Peter had probably already chewed them out for it.

A shout from up in the arena made her run for the stairs. Taking them two at a time, she burst into the large conference room the wedding party had been using as the bride's dressing room.

"What happened?" she panted, bending at the waist to catch her breath. Aidan was standing next to Claire, who was standing in front of an open empty closet.

"The dress and tux are gone. Murphy was supposed leave them and they're gone. I can't get a hold of Tande and I can't get a hold of Murphy. I'm going to kill them both!" Claire turned to Aidan, her eyes glassy with unshed tears. "She'll tank this business."

Aidan shook his head. "I'm sure there's a perfectly logical explanation."

"Marcus," Claire bit out.

Car doors slammed outside and the sounds of female voices filtered up the stairwell behind Anna. She stepped aside as DJ and her bridesmaids stomped into the conference room wearing shorts, tank tops, and their hair in messy buns.

"So this is happening today!" DJ announced, tossing her purse on the conference table and sinking into one of the padded chairs.

Claire masked her anxiety immediately, shoved the door to the closet closed, and smiled at DJ. "Are you ready for the big day?"

"I just bailed the groom out of jail. You tell me."

Anna covered her mouth before yet another laugh could escape. It shouldn't be funny. But this wedding had more kinks than a fifty-year-old stripper. The poor woman was about to get even more bad news. How did a wedding dress go missing, anyway?

"I'll call Dawn and Harmony. Between us we've got hands for each head of hair." That would solve one problem. The dress thing was Claire's. Anna didn't know how the wedding planner was going to make a dress appear from thin air.

"Thank you," DJ said, turning her chair to face Anna. "You are so sweet. You've been so good about letting us invade your ranch and take over."

Anna smiled. "It's going to be a wonderful day. Just wait till you get to the end. You'll laugh about all the hiccups one day."

"I sure hope so," DJ said.

Chapter Ten
by RL Syme

The drugs were wearing off and Tande could feel the nausea rising. Claire's texts were madly coming in, ever since Tande had found, and turned on, her phone. They may have been responsible for the nausea.

They ranged from *Where are you*, to *Where the hell are you*, to more profanity, to *You'd better not be where I think you are*, to *I swear to God, Tande* and various accouterments.

Among Claire's mad-texting was the one response Tande had typed out while standing at the desk at *Beautique* earlier.

I'm taking care of the dress and tux. Will be there soon.

"Are you sure we have to go to the ranch now?" Marcus broke their strange silence, staring at the road ahead of them.

"I have to get these things to Claire." Tande patted the bags on her lap.

"I could have taken them."

"It's my job, Marcus." Tande rubbed her free hand up and down the side of her face. Dr. Roe had told her she might still be in shock for a while, and touching would ground her. Of course, the good doctor had been looking at Marcus when she said that, and Tande was afraid he would take that as license to touch her.

She just needed to get through this wedding and back to Austin, in her nice warm bed, where she could cry and miss Marcus and mourn never seeing him again. But that was their fate. These last two days had proved, if nothing else, that she and Marcus were a disaster waiting to happen.

"You couldn't call it good on account of *felony*?" A hint of sarcasm laced

48

his voice and he squeezed the steering wheel.

"Claire is ready to shit a brick fireplace. I have to fix this." She tapped her fingers across the noisy plastic. "I will fix this."

"It wasn't your fault about the wedding dress. You didn't know he would steal it, or the tux."

Tande nodded. "I still have to fix it."

More silence, as the trees flashed by them on Sweet Mountain Road. The hospital had been tense, to say the least. Marcus had held her again, and Tande could have sworn the same feelings cropped up all over again. She felt closer to Marcus on that morning than she had in...years.

And all it took was a felony.

They approached the drive into the ranch and Marcus grabbed her hand. Tande didn't realize she'd jumped at his touch until he said, "Should I not do that?"

A bittersweet smile crept over her lips. "I don't want to get used to it."

His mouth slipped into a hard line. They were back to not talking about it, which suited Tande. At least they weren't naked, falling out of anyone's janitor closet. Although they might still make the tabloids. It wasn't everyday a wedding planner to the stars shot her assistant.

"Here we are," he said. "You want me to go upstairs with you?"

"I think I'll be..." Tande stopped when she saw the edge of the bale wall. It looked like the ranch hands had taken hay from the end, around the barn, and used it to patch up the middle. While the center looked passably untouched, it made both the ends shorter, which meant she could see both the barn and the pavilion from the road—something they had been trying to avoid with the construction of the wall in the first place.

The wall, as it stood, was useless. It would serve no one, standing as it was. But at least there wasn't a gaping hole in the middle, as Marcus had warned her.

"I'll wait here." Marcus rolled down the windows and turned off the car. "We still need to go into the station."

Tande side-eyed him. She still had to finish making her statement. It was only because Marcus was a deputy and Somewhere was a small town that they'd let her go at all. But she owed it to Claire to fix this.

"I'll be right back." She opened the door with her good arm and gathered up the *Beautique* bags.

"Don't you want some help with those?" He made to open his door.

"No." Tande gestured to his arm—in a matching sling to hers. "You only have one good arm."

"You, too."

"I know." She shrugged, trying to keep her nerves in her stomach, where they belonged. "But I can do it."

Tande carried the dresses inside and up the stairs. Each step made her shoulder throb a little, but she just kept thinking about her warm bed back in Austin, and how every step she took was carrying her one little bit closer to that kind of safety.

What she couldn't say to Marcus…what she feared telling him…was that if Claire saw him right now, she might murder him. She already blamed him for their debacle with the tabloids, and with DJ's ruined dress and Brent's ruined tux, and Murphy in the hospital… Tande just needed to face the music alone.

She knocked on the conference room door at the top of the stairs. So many voices squealed behind the door, she was afraid of what she might see if she opened the doors.

Harmony, the cute young ranch staffer, opened the door and her eyes went nuclear. "Oh my god, Tande." She immediately took the bags and pulled Tande inside the room.

Everyone buzzed at the sight of her. Claire's face, at first, crunched into anger, and then dropped to her sling. Her mouth dropped open and her hand went to cover it. She glanced up at Aidan and he anchored her shoulder in his grip.

In office chairs spread around the big room sat DJ, Emily, and Dixie. Each of them had someone standing over them with pieces of hair in their hands. But none of them were stylists. Anna, she recognized. The other staff, she didn't.

Tande wasn't even going to ask. After the monumental list of things that had gone wrong with this wedding. They still needed their final bill to get paid, after all.

"God, Tan, what happened?" Claire pulled away from Aidan, her face wrinkled in concern.

"I'd rather not talk about it." Tande dropped her voice. "I have to go back to the station, still."

Claire's eyes moved, expectant and wide, to the door. "Where's Murphy?"

Tande swallowed. "He won't be coming at all."

"Why?"

"He's in the hospital."

The entire room gasped in unison. Tande grimaced and handed Claire the dayplanner she'd been carrying around in her sling. "This has all the notes in it about the ceremony. I'll try to make it back in time for the first-look."

"Are you all right, Tande?" DJ held out her hand, while her head was stationery.

Tande walked to her chair and took the offered comfort. "I'm better. It was a long night."

"You're not going to tell us what happened because I'd really like to know why you're wearing my wedding dress?" DJ asked.

"Yeah, come on, we're dying with curiosity here." Emily leaned over to her friend with a hand over her mouth. "Is that blood?"

Claire opened the day-planner and thumbed through the documents. Her face was tight and drawn, and Tande couldn't quite make out the emotion.

"It must be bad if she has to go back to the police station," Aidan offered.

Tande threw him a grateful smile. "It's bad. But I don't want my mess to…" She couldn't say the words. Not after the other wedding debacle that was undoubtedly flashing through everyone's minds at the moment.

DJ let out a manic laugh. "Girl, I had to bail my groom out of jail this morning. I started drinking a looooooong time ago. Champagne helps."

Tande's mind flashed through the shooting, the hotel room, the ambulance, the hospital, the police station… she was pretty certain she could ruin the wedding with all that. Never mind tequila. She needed a forget-me-now pill. Maybe for everyone.

"Whatever happened, we'll get through it." Claire sniffed and came to stand beside her. "Whatever." She drilled Tande with a sincere stare. "Whatever."

"We're just glad you're all right." Aidan joined his fiancée. "I can help Claire with whatever needs doing until you get back."

"Yes, Aidan can give me whatever I need." Claire blushed when she'd had a moment to think about what she just said.

The two of them shared a glance that made Tande laugh out loud. They had sex-glow and they didn't even know it. But it lightened Tande's mood just a bit. She wouldn't mind some sex-glow of her own at the moment.

But Marcus didn't belong to her. Not the way Aidan belonged to Claire. Not the way he should, in order to fix her lack-of-a-sex-glow problem.

If she could just get through the day. *One foot in front of the other.*

"Do you need a ride to the station?" Aidan asked.

"Marcus is downstairs." Tande waved him off. "He gave me a ride from the hospital, and he said he'll bring me back."

She waited for Claire's response, but none came. Her blonde friend just kept flipping through documents. She may have gripped the dayplanner a little more ferociously than she had been, but she didn't make a comment about Marcus.

Thank God for small favors.

"What is this?" Harmony had unzipped the dress bag and was fingering the material, awe in her voice.

"DJ's new dress." Tande tried to sound excited, but she just couldn't bring herself to muster any enthusiasm. Nicole Bissette at *Beautique* had warned her that she only had one unclaimed dress in DJ's size, and it was one they'd been trying to sell for almost two years with no luck. It was too couture for Somewhere, apparently.

"And Brent's tux, I hope." Claire picked up the bottom of the dress bag and looked underneath it.

"Yes, and Brent's new tux." Tande refrained from adding details, since Nicole only had one tux in Brent's size, too. *I'm not a buy-the-same-day kind of place*, Nicole had warned. *Even sample dresses are usually spoken for, months in advance.*

Of course, that was part of the benefit of using *Beautique*. Everything was hand-made to order. But the ordering took weeks, at best. Months at worst. To walk in the door and expect a dress was unreasonable.

And yet, that was what she had done that morning. All while still wearing the beautiful dress DJ had painstakingly found after months of searching and then had tailored exactly the way she wanted it. DJ's beautiful, pink wedding dress that had been irrevocably ruined by Marcus's blood all over the bodice.

Tande only hoped she still had a job when they saw the extreme couture dress and the hipster tux. And when she had to tell DJ that her dress would never be coming back, because it was now in the police evidence locker.

Forget employed. She'd settle for alive.

Chapter Eleven
by Jodi Vaughn

"My God, it's beautiful." The words slipped past Emily's Smith's lips as she stood inside the barn at Saddles For Hope ranch where DJ and Brent's wedding was to be held.

So far, everything had gone wrong with this wedding, from the groom being arrested to the destroyed bridesmaids' dresses. But now standing where the ceremony would soon take place, Emily let the stress of all the mishaps roll off her shoulders. It looked too perfect for anything else to go wrong.

Rustic wood chairs with white cushions for guests lined the aisle of the barn in a V-formation. Grapevines decorated with greenery and tiny flowers draped to the floor between the chairs. Lanterns with white candles sat beside the chairs leading to the front where DJ and Brent would soon exchange vows to become husband and wife.

"If nothing else happens." Emily took a deep breath and walked down the aisle as her heels echoed on the old barn wood floor. Stopping at the other end of the barn door she peered out toward the horse trails, looking for Brent and DJ.

It was the first look for the soon-to-be married couple and the wedding photographer had suggested they take the pictures by the horse trails. The lush green hills and trees made for a perfect backdrop.

Except there was one little problem. So far there was nothing perfect about this wedding.

Her gaze immediately landed Brent and DJ dressed in completely different tuxes and gowns than what they had originally picked out for the wedding.

Even from this distance, Emily could see Brent fidgeting. Since both the wedding dress and the groom's tux had been destroyed, they'd had to get new outfits. They had only one option and it was a far cry from both DJ and Brent's style.

Brent held his arms out and looked down at his hipster tux and grimaced like he was wearing a clown suit. Claire called out instructions on how to stand and Brent mumbled something. Even from this distance, Emily could make out the curse word on his lips.

But the person she really felt bad for was DJ.

A wedding was something most little girls dreamed of. It was all about the bride and what she wanted. So when DJ's dressed had been ruined, they had hurried to find a replacement in her size. There was only one left and it had hung in the store for two years. The store owner called a one of a kind mermaid couture wedding gown.

DJ said it looked like a European hooker's dress.

Emily tried to stifle a giggle and failed, as DJ fisted her arms at her side and glared at the wedding photographer who was busy trying to give her instructions on how to stand.

The form fitting lace dress had long sleeves and a sheer lace panel in the front that flared out at the knees to the ground. The plunging neckline was daring and Emily knew DJ wasn't comfortable exposing so much boob. What really made the dress bad, was the white floor length satin cape that was heavy and hot.

"What's so funny?" Derrek's voice had her turning around to face him. He had Tatum with him, who looked past her at Brent and DJ.

"Sorry." She slapped a hand over her mouth and tried not to laugh. "I mean I'm tired and haven't eaten. I'm stressed from everything that's happened. I'm a little punch drunk."

He frowned and peered over her shoulder. A lazy smile settled on his lips. "Yeah, at least I'm not getting blamed for this one." He pulled her against his side to watch his sister give the wedding photographer hell about keeping on the cape.

"What's she bitching about?" Tatum asked.

Emily watched intently. The photographer was in front of DJ, making her hold her arms out and telling her to catch the edge of the cape between her fingers. Yards of satin fanned out on either side of her.

DJ shook her head, let the cape slip through her fingers and glared.

"She's looks like an albino peacock." Derrek chuckled.

She elbowed him. "That's not funny. And for God's sake don't even say that to her face." She turned and looked at him. The sight of him in the black tux sent a jolt of desire through her stomach.

"I like the way you're looking at me." Derrek cupped her face with the palm of his large hand and brought her in for a kiss.

"Get a room," Tatum snarked. "I'm going outside to wait on the brides maids."

She parted her lips as Tatum disappeared. He kissed her hard and deep.

Emily groaned and forced herself to pull away. "We don't need to start something we can't finish."

"Who says we aren't finishing this?" He pulled her into his chest.

"Derrek. Stop." She giggled and pushed against his chest. "You'll get my dress all wrinkled."

He took her hands in his and stepped back to let his gaze drift down her body. "You look beautiful." His eyes softened as he spoke and her heart tripped.

"Thank you. I happened to luck out on my dress. While all the bridesmaid's dresses are pink, they are not the same shade of pink. And they don't match." She sighed with relief as the image of poor Dixie's dress popped in her head.

"Yikes. How did DJ take that?"

"Better than how she reacted to her own dress." Emily shook her head. "But I'm looking on the bright side. We made it through the worst. The two super fans are still locked up so nothing else can go wrong, right?" She looked up into Derrek's eyes for the reassurance she needed.

"Right. It only gets better from here." Derrek turned as Brent and DJ entered the barn. DJ had a glass of champagne clutched in her hand. She stopped, down the drink and motioned for Brent to fill it up again.

Derrek smiled, walked over to DJ, and kissed her on the cheek. "You look beautiful, sis."

DJ's scowl didn't soften whatsoever. "I do not." She plucked at the lace sleeves as a sheen of sweat covered her upper lip. "I'm hot as hell and I look like some kind of colorless peacock."

"Hey, that's what I told Emily." Derrek brightened.

DJ glared at her brother and socked him in the arm.

"Ignore him, babe." Brent took her by the hand and pulled her away from her brother. Smart thinking, because DJ could throw a punch like nobody's business. They didn't have time to get another wedding dress if she ended up on the floor wrestling her brother.

"Look at me." Brent took DJ's face between his palms. "I don't care what you wear." His eyes dipped to the plunging neckline, "Although I am liking how that dress looks on you."

DJ looked like she was ready to hit Brent too.

Brent wised up and looked into her eyes. "What I'm trying to say is, I don't care what you wear, you could wear a potato sack and rock it."

DJ's eyes softened slightly.

"All I care about is standing in front of our friends and family and hearing you say you'll still be my wife. I want the world to know I'm yours and you belong to me."

That's all it took.

DJ smiled and launched herself at Brent, who caught her in his arms. The couple kissed like they hadn't seen each other in forever.

"Ahem." The photographer cleared her throat as she hurried into the room. "We must get the rest of these photos done before the guests arrive." She turned, and her gaze landed on Emily. "How long until the rest of the bridesmaids and groomsmen arrive?"

"They're all outside," Claire announced as she hurried down the aisle with Aidan. "Go ahead and get pictures of the couple and I'll get the rest of the wedding party herded inside."

DJ rolled her eyes and Brent let out a sigh as they made their way to where they would soon be taking their vows.

"I'll help." Aidan made his way down the aisle.

Claire turned to leave, but stopped when she saw Emily. "You stay right here. In fact sit." She pointed to one of the chairs. "I refuse to let anything else happened today and the last thing I need is disappearing bridesmaids."

"Where would I go?"

Claire leaned in so only Emily could hear. "I have no idea. It's like the freaking Bermuda Triangle of all weddings with all this crazy going on."

Emily shook her head but obeyed. Claire had certainly been under a lot of stress with this wedding so she could understand where the woman was coming from.

She walked over to the chair on the front row and sat. The chair swayed for a second and then collapsed in a heap on the ground.

"Oh, Emily." DJ ran over with her cape flapping behind her. "Are you okay?"

"What happened? What was that noise?" Claire came running down the aisle her face pinched tight.

"The chair fell when Emily sat down," DJ said.

A bit dazed, she accepted Derrek's help up. "I'm okay, just embarrassed." Her face heated.

"Here, sit down here." Derrek guided her to a chair on the opposite side of the aisle to sit.

She gave him a smile as she eased herself into the chair. The chair buckled but Derrek was fast and grabbed her up before she could land on the floor a second time.

"What the hell?" Brent frowned.

"The chairs." Claire's face went white and she held out her hands. "No one touch the chairs. I bet they've been tampered with by those crazy chicks of yours, Brent."

DJ glared.

"They're not my chicks. But they *are* crazy." He held up his hands in defense.

"Derrek, go grab the ranch hands outside and have them sit in every chair," Claire barked out.

Derrek nodded and took off outside.

"Don't worry, DJ. I'm going to take care of this," Claire assured her.

"Yeah, but we don't know what else those crazy women sabotaged." Emily frowned and rubbed her sore butt.

"Be straight with me, Emily," DJ said. "Is this karma trying to tell me this is a mistake? Because I could leave. I could walk out and leave right now. At this point I don't think anyone would even miss me. "

Emily turned to her friend and smiled. "Honey, that's the champagne talking."

DJ shook her head. "And the missing groom, and the ruined dresses, and the death threats."

"Do you love Brent?"

"Of course I do."

"And I know he loves you." Emily squeezed DJ's hand. "I think if you two can weather all this and still stand strong, then you and Brent are meant to be."

Chapter Twelve
by Krystal Shannan

"Leave this office immediately. I don't want to see your face for at least twenty-four hours. And if I ever hear of any more hazing or unlawful arrests in this office, it will go on everyone's permanent record. Is that clear?" Allan VonBrandt hissed the last few words through gritted teeth. They were an embarrassment to the department. Arresting someone without any evidence. Brent, was a well-known celebrity and a personal friend. Wally was slightly daft, but he'd made it through the training. There was no reason for this level of incompetence.

Jeff, however, should be ashamed of himself.

Allan turned to look down at Jeff and scowled. It took everything inside him not to growl in the man's face. "You will do every scrap of paperwork Wally has on his desk and anything that comes across his desk for the next month in addition to your own. Is that clear?"

The deputy grimaced and nodded, not daring to speak.

"I don't suppose I have to remind you what kind of liability you've opened the department to. With everything going down around Randall, the last thing any of us needs is more investigation into this office. I'm not sure about you, but I would very much like to keep my position here at the Sheriff's department."

"Yes, sir. I would. There won't ever be another issue. I guarantee." Jeff said, swallowing audibly.

Allan narrowed his gaze and grunted before walking across the office to rejoin the County Commissioner and JJ Walker, where they stood much closer to Edna's desk than he would've preferred.

She was busy digging through the file cabinet behind her desk, not paying any attention to the two men chatting away, but Allan knew better. Anything said within earshot of Edna was as good as printing on the front page of the local paper.

"Allan, everything squared away?" JJ asked, rubbing his chin.

"Yes," he answered. "Let's talk in the sheriff's office for privacy." He gestured toward the back of the building. Randall's office wouldn't afford much privacy, but at least it had enclosed walls and a door.

The two men nodded and walked ahead of him passed the deputies' desks. He shut the door behind them and turned to see JJ Walker sink into Randall's desk chair. *Guess that answers the question of interim sheriff. Hart must've told them no.*

"A decision has been made, Deputy VonBrandt," the commissioner started. "The other commissioners and I feel that while the investigation into the department is going on, having someone from outside as the interim sheriff will be beneficial for everyone."

Allan rolled his head to the side, enjoying the sound of his vertebrae popping and JJ Walker's mouth pressing tighter and tighter with each crack. Even the commission had fallen silent, waiting for him to what…get angry? Blow a fuse? He intended to be sheriff of this town one day, but he wanted to be elected and earn it. Putting JJ Walker in as interim didn't bother him in the slightest, but it was fun to see them squirm.

They knew he was the man behind keeping this department running and had been for years. Nothing could be done about Randall until he'd finally hung himself on his own words. Now progress could be made. This department needed better structure. More employees. A detective unit would go a long way as well, but that would be something he could push for in an election. The town had grown and needed the additional team.

"Sounds like a smart move, Commissioner," Allan said, reaching out.

The commissioner shook his hand and before speaking. "Well, good. Then…Excellent. Glad to have your support, VonBrandt."

"This town means everything to my family and myself. I would always want the best for it," Allan answered, flashing a disarming smile. He needed the commissioners on his side when he ran for the position this fall.

JJ Walker could be interim, a babysitter, while the town got its shit together.

But he would be sheriff of Somewhere, Texas.

His life would continue on the path he'd set out for and it would be bigger than the secret his family hid. Being a werewolf wasn't *who* he was. It was just something that allowed him to do his job a little better than anyone else.

"If that's all then, I should get back to work. There're a couple of people just coming through the front door," he said, smiling again and slipping out of Randall's office. He heard them both comment that they hadn't heard anything, but sure enough, Deputy Edison and Tande Walker were coming through the front door as he closed the office one behind him. *Great. All I need is her daddy stepping into this and making a bigger mess.*

He raised a hand, catching Edison's attention, and nodded his head toward the hallway leading to the two interrogation rooms. Edison slipped his hand down Tande's back and powerwalked them both across the office, leaving Edna once again with nothing to eavesdrop on.

He grabbed a folder from the top of his desk and fell into step behind them.

"Get in here before your dad and the commissioner come out of Randall's office."

"Shit," Tande cursed under her breath.

The poor woman had been through hell over the last twelve hours. Allan couldn't help but feel sorry for both of them. They should be resting. Marcus had been shot and Tande had shot the bastard who abducted them both. Although, Marcus shouldn't have been on the job anyway, with the personal connection he had with Tande, but it didn't matter.

Allan just needed her statement and then he could tidy up this mess and forget it ever happened. Kidnapping. Attempted murder.

By the gods, this town needed a detective unit so he didn't have to personally field every crazy and convoluted situation that reared its ugly head.

He closed the interrogation room door just as the creak of Randall's office door echoed across the large room. *Close. Now if Edna will keep her trap shut.* Allan stood next to the door, listening to the people outside.

Marcus and Tande threw him an odd glance as they sat at the table next to each other and waited, but he ignored them both.

The commissioner and JJ bid Edna a good day and she did the same without mentioning Tande's presence in the building.

A grateful sigh slipped from between his lips and he snapped his attention to the two people at the table —both sporting bloodhound-sized bags under their eyes.

"I need your written statements," Allan said, sliding a pen and paper toward each of them before he sat in the chair on the other side of the table.

"Am I..." Tande started, but couldn't finish. The stress of everything was eating at her. Her hands were shaking and her pulse was all over the place. She probably wouldn't sleep well for a couple of weeks.

Marcus shifted in his chair uncomfortably, his pulse steady, but his breathing heavy. He was stressed and exhausted. Allan knew Edison wanted to assure her everything would be fine, but it wasn't his place. Marcus had chosen to turn in his badge and his gun and operate through this mess as a civilian without telling anyone what was actually going on.

"Ms. Walker. I need your signed, written statement. And yours, Edison. Then you're both free to go. I'll take care of everything. You were defending yourself. It's pretty cut and dry, ma'am." He gave her a reassuring wink. "Don't you have a wedding to be at?"

Chapter Thirteen
by Becca Boyd

Aidan Conley had been ordered to destroy the wedding cake. There were no two ways of hearing the words his fiancée had said to him. *Eat some of the cake, only make it look like you didn't.*

"How the hell am I supposed to make it look like I haven't eaten any of the cake?" he found himself saying aloud. One of the ranch boys stuffed a meatball into his mouth and shot Aidan a side-eye glance.

"She said to test everything," the kid said.

Aidan waved him off. He didn't care about somebody stealing a damn meatball. He was supposed to ruin this cake in a tasteful way. He wasn't a food critic, he was a firefighter, dammit.

"Just stick your finger in the back and then cover it up," the kid said around the remains of his meatball.

Aidan looked at where he pointed. The five-tier pink monster of a cake was nearly in the middle of the big round table that had been set up for the express purpose of displaying the sugar bomb. Sure, Meg had made it, but it was a nightmare. Too much pink, too much frosting.

Maybe that would save him in the end. He stuck his knuckle into the base and came away with a finger full of sugar. But when he put it in his mouth, it wasn't as sickly sweet as he expected. It had a tangy, surprising flavor and a little bit of a sweet kick, like lemonade.

He wiped his finger on his t-shirt and used his other hand to swipe at the frosting so it looked at least a little smooth. You could still tell it had been messed with, but better safe than sorry.

"Is it bad that I just realized we're guinea pigs?" he asked the staffer.

The boy's eyes went wide. "What do you mean?"

"You know why she's having us taste the food, right?"

The kid shook his head. He'd somehow gotten his hands on another meatball and Aidan could see the remnants when the staffer said, "You don't think they poisoned it, do you?"

Aidan shrugged. "That's why she told you to taste it."

"In case it killed me?" The kid went pale. "What if I really die?"

"You're not gonna die. It's just a precaution."

He pulled two more meatballs out of his pocket and walked around to the side of the pavilion. With a wind-up, he heaved the potentially deadly food into the woods.

"The food isn't poisoned," Aidan said. "The women were in jail when the food was made."

"But not the cake?"

"Nope." Aidan went around the table. "What do you think? Is it ruined?"

The kid followed and shook his head. "It doesn't look too bad. You didn't get any cake, though. Just the icing."

Aidan sighed. He was right. That bite had been all lemon. But he couldn't just eat the cake. Aidan left the kid looking for an easy way to desecrate DJ's wedding cake and went looking for Claire.

If he dropped dead on the way to the barn, at least the cake would be intact.

They ought to have been playing *Foggy Mountain Breakdown* in the background while Claire made the staff run through the barn sitting in chairs to see if they'd fall. They bobbed up and down and moved from chair to chair, and when one would find a wobbly seat, they'd run it back to another crew who waited at the back with some replacement screws Anna Granger had provided.

They were fixing and praying and jumping, and it felt like a little urgent banjo music should accompany them. Claire's face was so stern and steadfast. She watched each of her helpers and kept one eye on the hyperventilating bride outside taking pictures in her heavy dress.

Someone smart had managed to figure out a way to get the cape off without ruining the dress. DJ's makeup had been sagging in the heat, and Emily's chair had broken the last camel's back.

No one was saying it out loud, but everyone expected either the bride or the groom to bolt at any moment. They might have kept a truck running if it wasn't set to go up like a tinder box around this place. And if there hadn't already been one fire.

"Can I talk to you for a minute?" Aidan thumbed at the pavilion, coming up beside Claire.

She didn't move. "Did you taste the cake?"

"I tasted the frosting. I couldn't figure out how to eat some of the cake without basically destroying it."

"Just destroy the back. I don't care. I want to make sure it's real cake and it didn't get replaced by horseshit or something."

Aidan couldn't stifle the laugh. "Who's gonna frost a bunch of shit and send it to a wedding?"

Claire almost always cracked a tiny smile at even the lamest of his jokes. This time, not even a memory of a smile. She was too focused.

"Aidan…"

"Okay, okay." He put up defensive hands. "I'll ruin the cake."

"Don't ruin it too bad." She swiped her hand on her jean shorts. "It still has to look pretty for the wedding."

"Do we have a backup plan if I die?"

But that joke got him even less of a smile than the first one had. She was just not going to lighten up. And he couldn't use the proposal card. He'd done that in the midst of a stress attack on Monday. You could only do that once.

Aidan checked his phone. It was late. Later than he'd realized. "We're supposed to be out of the barn here in about ten minutes so they can start seating people, aren't we?"

She looked at his phone and winced. "The pictures aren't done yet, let alone the chairs. We still have to light the candles, and Tande's not back. I haven't changed…"

He caught her wrist and pulled her into his arms. She struggled against him at first, but after a moment, she just laid her head on his chest. Aidan stroked the back of her head. Years of fighting fires had taught him that everyone had a breaking point, and sometimes, a few breaths could be the difference between a crisis and a solution. "Just breathe. People will wait," he said.

Claire filled her lungs and then pushed the breath out, fast. "People shouldn't have to wait."

"You can't help that. Just let them finish. Go get your dress on." He kissed her forehead and sent her toward the arena. "I'll go taste the cake."

She leaned back in his arms and looked up at him. The air caught in his throat. Claire was so damn beautiful. He pushed her hair along her cheek and behind her ear and lowered his lips to hers.

The movement of her tongue under his reminded him of the last time she got this stressed out. He'd pulled the car over. But there was no pulling the car over tonight. They were on a crash course with this wedding and had no brakes.

"Go taste the cake," she whispered against his lips.

"I will." Aidan hopped to a quick step and hot-footed it out of the barn.

"Hope you don't die, baby," she called after him.

Aidan laughed his way back to the pavilion. At least Claire was laughing again. That was a good sign, because it looked like Marcus and Tande had just pulled up to the parking lot.

If Marcus knew what was good for him, he'd high-tail it before Claire saw him. That was one crisis Claire wouldn't be able to laugh her way through. And there might be an attempted murder to cap off the wedding, after all.

Chapter Fourteen
by R L Syme

Marcus would never be able to drive past Saddles for Hope again without thinking of the fire that had started this whole mess. He'd seen the smoke and known that all the hope Tande had placed in this wedding were about to burn away in the July wind.

Even parking in the lot reminded him of that moment.

He tried to run around and get Tande's door. She'd been moving slow since the hospital. He ignored his shoulder as much as possible, although it was harder to ignore the sling.

She climbed out of the Jeep before he could get to her. Marcus was surprised at how much that bothered him.

"You don't have to stay," she said, sliding against the door.

"You asked me to come to the wedding."

"But, y'know, as a guest." Tande licked her bottom lip.

"You want me to go now?" He came to stand against the car beside her. Maybe the side-by-side thing wouldn't be as intimidating. She seemed to be pulling away more, now that her shock was wearing off.

She didn't want him to be near as much as she had that morning.

"I should change into my dress." Tande touched his arm. "You don't have to stay. Don't you want to go get some other clothes on?"

Marcus looked down at his clothing for the first time in hours. They'd taken Brent's tux off Murphy at the hospital, but he had been wearing his bloody jeans for hours after that. They'd given him a clean shirt after they sewed up his shoulder, but even that looked dingy already.

It had been a long day.

"You don't think they'll want me wearing my gym shorts at the wedding?" He tried to put a touch of humor in his voice, but found it hard.

Every moment felt like goodbye with Tande, now that it was time for the wedding to start. Time for her job to start. Time for her to go back to Austin.

Marcus didn't want to think about that at the moment.

"Let me come with you, just in case you need help." He pushed off the Jeep and walked after her.

Tande didn't rise to the occasion, which made a little lump in the pit of his stomach. She always rose to the occasion. This particular occasion, she should have told him to go home, get his suit on, and get back for the wedding, because if he followed her upstairs to a private dressing room where she was about to get naked, they couldn't be trusted.

That was what he wanted her to say.

A crash sounded from the direction of the barn, and Marcus instinctively reached for his service weapon. But it wasn't there. He'd turned it in.

The profile of a wiry young man holding out his arms inside the barn made Marcus keep walking. He couldn't see exactly what had happened, but someone was trying to calm the edgy crowd, at least.

Marcus would rather stick to Tande, as close as he could stay.

She didn't speak the whole way to the conference room, but when they reached the door, she held it open for him. "Would you like to go in and check it out, so you can go home?"

He chewed on his lip, trying not to say the thing that kept coming to his mind. *She should be at home.* At his home, preferably. In bed, sleeping, drinking, forgetting. Not working.

There were plenty of things they could do in bed that didn't require the use of their injured limbs. Sleeping came to mind, among others.

"I would like for us to talk."

Tande shook her head and walked into the room when he wouldn't. "I don't want to talk."

But she didn't go all the way in. She froze in the door and Marcus ran into her when he tried to follow. Tande wasn't speaking or moving, and his protective instinct flared. He put his hand on her waist. She still didn't budge.

"You could knock." Claire's voice split the tension with a big anvil of awkward. Without any warning, the past had come to sit on Marcus's chest.

He already felt bad enough about the part he played in ruining the other wedding, and this one hadn't been his fault, but he still felt the guilt.

Claire zipped up a fitted mint green dress and glared at him with years of frustration threatening to spill out behind her eyes. "You shouldn't be here," she said.

Marcus put up his good hand. "I was just making sure Tande was safe."

"Of course you were." The bite in Claire's voice could have drawn blood.

"You can go, Marcus."

He couldn't stand the resignation Tande displayed. Her shoulders slumped, her tone quiet, eyes down. If she hadn't been injured, he would have shaken her.

"Tan, what are you doing? This isn't you." He swept his hand down her body. "You're no coward."

Tears shimmered in her gaze and she shook her head. "Don't. Please."

He stepped past her, fueled by all the frustration he'd been holding back since Tande had done his job for him that morning and shot a psycho. One finger came up and he shook it at Claire. "This is not her fault. Look, I get that this wedding is a disaster. But you can't be mad at her for this."

"I'm not." The tiny blonde set her jaw. "I'm mad at you."

Marcus reeled. "Me? How can you be mad at me?"

Claire advanced on him. "How can I not? You two have this...volatile thing that happens when you're around each other. And you won't give it up. You keep saying you will, but you don't."

He couldn't respond. She wasn't wrong. Marcus ground his teeth and tried to pretend he wasn't still in love with Tande. If he wasn't even fooling Claire, why did he think he could fool anyone? Himself included.

"The world gets caught up in your orbit and somehow, you destroy it, every time you're together. Forget the weddings, forget my career, forget Tande's career or anything fleeting like that." She sighed and pointed at Tande. "You ruin her, too. And she ruins you. You can't stay apart, but because you're both too stubborn to sacrifice, you can't be together, either."

Those words hung in the air for a long time. They all knew it was true, and had been true for years.

"You need to make a decision, once and for all," Claire said. "And then you need to move on with your lives."

Tande's back straightened and her head snapped up. "I've had the day from hell, Claire. I don't need ultimatums from you."

Marcus wanted to smile. That was his girl, finally. She had a fire that would always burn, and would always consume. And he loved her for it.

It was Claire's turn to fall back on her heels.

"I'm not doing this anymore." Tande crossed the room and picked up the last remaining hangar bag. "I need to get dressed so we can finish this day."

She walked into the hall and Marcus made to follow her. Claire's hand on his arm stopped him.

"You see that, don't you? I can't tell you how many times I've told her she needs to move on and get over you." Claire released him and crossed her arms. "And that's the response I get every time."

Marcus watched Tande slip into the bathroom with her dress. She had this simple grace. She managed to look beautiful even in the old cutoffs and the too-big T-shirt Candace Roe had lent her. She'd looked beautiful in the bloody wedding dress. But more than that, she was his other half.

"I know how she feels." Marcus took the chair behind him and drew one hand over his head. "I don't want to think about her being gone from my life."

"But you won't just follow her?"

"My family..."

"Will always be here. And Austin is only two hours away."

He took a deep breath. "My job..."

"You'll find a job in Austin." Claire touched his shoulder and the compassion shook Marcus's resolve. "You know she can't come back here."

"She finally told me." A weight settled in his throat and he tried not to think about what she'd told him in that closet about her family. To be unwanted...to feel unloved and unwelcome...he wanted her never to feel that again. Ever.

"You love her. I know that," Claire said. "You're not the only one."

"I don't know if I can just leave here." Marcus swallowed hard against the lump. "My life is here."

"Your life will go with you."

A knock at the door had Marcus looking up desperately, hoping to see Tande. Wouldn't he always be looking for her? If he let her go again, this might be the last time for her.

Aidan's grin disarmed the tension. "Well, babe, the cake didn't kill me yet." His eyebrows went up when he saw Marcus. "Hey, man. I figured you'd gone already."

"I need to get down there." Claire stopped to kiss Aidan. "Thank you for letting me take your life into my hands."

"Anything for you." Aidan's smile was playful, but Marcus saw something true underneath it. He really meant it.

"Did you fix the cake?" Claire straightened Aidan's tie.

"I left the ranch hand to do it. He said he had a plan. It's really not bad at all."

"Famous last words." The little laugh in Claire's voice lifted the rest of the tension. She glanced back at Marcus. "If you love her, you love her. If you don't, be done with her, please. I don't have the stamina to do this again, with you two."

"I know you need to go." Marcus waved at her. "I won't be in your way."

Marcus wasn't certain, but he thought he detected a flash of sadness on Claire's face as she left. Was she sad that he was going to let Tande go to Austin and not follow her?

She wasn't the only one.

Chapter Fifteen
by Emma Roman

Anna sat alone at one of the large round dinner tables under the pavilion. The toasts to the bride and groom had been made. Dinner was finished. Music had started and most people were swaying slowly in the dance area to a slow country ballad. Even the sun was starting to slip behind the tree-lined horizon. The scent of pine hung in the air along with the smell of the delicious meatballs and the luscious bite of alcohol.

A sigh slipped from her lips and she reclined in her chair. After everything that'd happened to this poor wedding, DJ and Brent's ceremony had been lovely, the food was delicious, and none of the guests had crashed to the floor in a sabotaged chair they'd missed. It was a win.

She sipped her white wine as a light breeze blew through the curls piled on top of her head. Dancing at her best friends' wedding last year led to a one-night stand, so this year she was keeping her butt planted in the chair and denying the crowd of good-looking guys a chance to entice her to do otherwise.

So far she'd only had to fend off someone's uncle with a mustache that reminded her of a fuzzy caterpillar. That "no" hadn't been hard. The second and third requests had come from a couple of handsome men she'd never met. They'd been a little more difficult to say no to, but her wine was keeping content and happy. No need for a man tonight that she would regret in the morning.

A loud whinny from the side of the pavilion caught her off guard and she rose from her chair. Two male voices were hollering "Cheeky, come

71

back!" and a second later her female paint, one of her best therapy horses, came trotting across the lawn to her left, straight for the pavilion. In addition to seemingly always knowing what the therapy patient in sessions needed, Cheeky, as she was known on the ranch, was amazingly adept at escaping from just about any enclosure.

Anna kicked off her heels and darted around the edge of the pavilion to try and head off the horse. Those boys were way behind and the mare was headed straight for the crowd. That horse loved people and she loved sugar. DJ's wedding cake was probably calling to her sweet tooth like a wailing siren.

"Cheeky," she hissed under her breath and raised an arm.

The mare snorted and side-stepped, trotting around her.

Crap!

The horse went right up into the crowded pavilion and wove her way through the tables, straight toward the cake. Several laughs and a few female squeals weren't far behind Cheeky's entrance.

Michael and Jeremy paused beside her to catch their breath.

"You stop her from getting that cake and get her back in the barn," she said, practically growling at them. Of all things that could happen, one of her horses eating the wedding cake was not going to be one of them.

"Yes, ma'am!" They took off at a run after the mare. Jeremy caught up to her first and clipped a lead to her halter while shoving a palm filled with sugar cubes under her muzzle.

Thank goodness.

"Cheeky wanted to congratulate the newlyweds," Jeremy called out, chuckling loudly and using that smooth bass voice of his to make it sound like the horse's appearance was planned all along. "But she'll be coming along with me now," he continued.

The crowd laughed and clapped. The music started again as the boys led the horse off the dance floor and away from the party.

Anna shook her head, releasing a large breath she hadn't realized she'd been holding onto. Crisis averted. The party would continue without interruption and she just needed to grab her shoes and head back to her little cabin for the night –possibly with one of the unopened bottles of wine behind the bar table.

They wouldn't mind sharing just one.

Chapter Sixteen
by KC Klein

DJ watched the three tiered cake wobble to the right. Then to the left. And for a second, the pink sugared art of perfection was maybe going to right itself and do what it was supposed to do, which was stay upright and look pretty.

But it didn't. Over twenty pounds of sugar, flour, and only lord knows how much pink food coloring went crashing to the floor in a pile of powdery, fondant mess.

She didn't move. Didn't even react. Just stood there with what might've been her ninth glass of champagne in her hand, in a wedding dress that would've made Elvira proud, next to her new husband who looked like a mobster straight out of the Rat Pack, and stared down at her once beautiful, perfect cake now splattered all over the floor.

Someone gasped. At this point it may have been Brent. Lord knew, it wasn't her. She was too far past surprise. Way past even shock. She was now firmly in the place of acceptance. Wasn't that the first of the twelve steps?

Lord grant me the serenity to accept the things I cannot change,
The courage to change the things I can,
And the wisdom to know the difference.

And this time was one of them. She threw back the last of her champagne—the AAs would be proud—dropped the knife in middle of the pink mess and walked out.

She didn't care if Brent followed. Didn't care how it looked that the bride had left in the middle of her reception. Could not have cared less that when she stepped outside her nightmare of a cape was dragged through the gift offerings of that damn paint horse that had traipsed through the barn earlier.

The only thing she cared about was getting home, getting out of this dress, and crawling into bed where she could cry herself to sleep for the next week.

"Babe, Babe! Wait up. Come on, wait up."

It was Brent. He was chasing her. Well, she didn't want to be caught. She hiked the front of her mermaid dress of chiffon and lace up past her knees, and broke into a sprint the best she could.

Brent was quicker. Must be because he could run and not just fast baby-step.

He caught her from behind, wrapping his arms around her waist, keeping them upright when she lost her footing, almost bringing them both down.

"Brent, no." She struggled in his arms. "Just let me go. I need to be left alone."

"No way." He pulled her close, his lips seeking his favorite spot on her neck. "There's no way I'm letting you run out on your...*our* wedding. We're not going to end tonight like this."

Maybe it was the effect of being up for close to twenty-four hours, maybe it was the stress of having everything that could go wrong go wrong, or more than likely, it was the finishing off an entire bottle of champagne herself. But she'd reached her breaking point. "I'm done, Brent. I'm done. I think God has been against us from the beginning. I think karma, the universe, or whatever you want to call it is trying to tell us something. This is not going to work."

Brent stiffened behind her. "What exactly do you mean by *this*?"

She turned in his arms. This time he let her. "*This.*" She gestured back and forth between the both of them, her hand cutting air already thick with tension. "*This* as in *this* marriage. *This* life. How can any marriage survive a wedding from hell at its foundation?"

Night had come up fast, but even with only the lights from the barn, DJ could see Brent's jaw twitch. He began deep inhaling through his nose that DJ recognized as his pissed-off-as-all-hell breathing.

Her stomach tightened into an alcohol soaked knot. She didn't want to fight with Brent, but someone needed to state the obvious.

He shook his head. "I can't believe what I'm hearing. I can't believe you want to call our marriage off because of a few mishaps during the wedding."

"Mishaps? Mishaps!" DJ's voice had reached that *watch-out-she's-hysterical* level, but she couldn't help it. She was angry and heart sick and scared, all at the same time. She'd always been too practical to be superstitious, but even she couldn't deny that the world had turned against them. She grabbed his hands and tried to make him understand. "It was more than a few mishaps. Horrible things happened, Brent. People were shot. My wedding gown is part of an actual criminal investigation. I can't think of one thing that has gone right. Not one thing has happened to give me hope that our marriage isn't doomed."

He took a step back and punched his fists into his pants pockets looking for the world like a pissed off Frank Sinatra. "So, is that what you think this means? That our marriage is doomed because the wedding was a disaster? So what? Big deal. This wedding has nothing to do with us. And I hate to break it to you babe, but the success, or failure, of our marriage has everything to do with how we handle right now and nothing to do with the actual wedding. Today is just one day in a row of a thousand days. When we're old and gray we'll look back on tonight and laugh. No one will believe us. This will be fodder for interviews for years to come."

He was trying to make her smile, but she didn't feel like smiling. Instead, her eyes filled with tears. She quickly turned around so Brent wouldn't see her wiping her eyes. What was the point of keeping her make-up on now? "Brent, it's not supposed to be this hard. It can't be."

"Who says? Who says it's not supposed to be hard. That's what marriage is. It's hard work, sacrifice, disappointment, and God, sometimes even painful."

She whirled on him. Couldn't he see she was trying to save them both from exactly that? "Then why in God's name would anyone get married? Why would we put ourselves through that kind of misery when we could just walk away now and save ourselves the heartache?"

He grabbed her by the arms, but the gentleness of before had passed. Instead, she felt the intensity that was all Brent. The passion that had driven him to beat all the odds and become one of today's fastest rising country stars. The absolute determination that had him convinced they could make a life together. "Because it's also beautiful, wonderful, breathtaking, and totally worth it. I don't want to go through all of the bad stuff either. No one does. But sometimes that's life, and if so, then there's no one else I'd rather have by my side than you."

DJ resisted the urge to fall into his gaze and shore up under his embrace. He'd convinced her before with his eyes, his damn sexy grin. Had wooed her with words and a damn love song on the radio.

Over the past few months, she'd never been happier. It hadn't mattered that there were times he'd holed up in the bunkhouse and only came out for meals and periodic showers. It hadn't mattered that she had her ranch that kept her busy, at times from dawn to dusk. It had just been good to know he was there. Within walking distance and that he was hers.

She chose the cowardly way instead, lowering her head and twisting her diamond ring that was big enough to sparkle even in the barn's flood lights. "I'm scared, Brent. What if this doesn't work out?"

What she really wanted to say was if their marriage didn't work out—if she had to say goodbye to another person that she loved—she didn't think her heart could take it.

Everyone thought she was so strong. Fearless and stubborn. And she was all those things. But she was also still that young girl who had sat on the couch and peered out the front window waiting for her parents to pull into the driveway.

She could take not loving, but she couldn't take loving and losing again.

Brent's face softened as he pulled her in close, resting his chin on top of her head. "Babe, there's no guarantee. No promise that can't be broken. All I can tell you is I love you. You're the reason I look forward to waking up in the morning and you're the reason I have a smile on my face when I go to sleep at night. I am prepared to do everything in my power to make sure you never regret walking back into that barn with me, but I need something from you also."

She closed her eyes. Her arms slipped underneath his tux coat and found his waist. She loved the feeling of strength that flowed from him into her. Inside his embrace was the only place she'd ever felt safe. Funny how she'd forgotten something so important and that it had taken a wedding tragedy for her to remember. "What?"

"Fight. Fight for us. I've never seen anyone battle as hard as you for the things that you love. And let me tell you sweetheart, we're gonna need some of that grit because it's not always gonna be easy. We're both stubborn and determined and both of us are used to getting our own way. So make *us* the something that you fight for, not run from. Can you do that?"

DJ nodded, not trusting her voice to actually say the words. She'd always been pragmatic to a fault. Brent was the one with faith. Maybe that was why they were so good together.

He kissed her on her head. "Besides, you're not really good at reading omens."

She pulled away and looked up at him. His brown eyes held a secret wink just for her. "What do you mean?"

Brent smiled that grin that had thousands of women falling head over heels in love with him—her included. "All the horrible things that have happened are not bad signs, they're good."

She narrowed her eyes trying to figure out if this was one of the tall tales he had a habit of telling.

"Haven't you heard? The worst weddings make the best marriages."

"Is that so?" Her good humor had started to come back. If they could weather this catastrophe, they could weather anything.

"Oh, sure," he said turning her in his arms and escorting her slowly back to the reception. "Besides, that's a great title for my next single."

"What? *The Wedding from Hell.*"

"Hmmm, something more original."

"Or *I Divorced My Husband The Day I Married Him.*

"Or…" A hinted smile on his lips. "How about *This Will Last, Despite The Woman I Married.*"

DJ punched him in the arm, but she was too tired to put any heat behind it. Instead, she snuggled in closer and wondered how much longer they'd have to stay until she could get her husband home and alone in their bed.

That was how Tande and Claire found them—arms around each other, enjoying one of those rare moments of marital bliss.

Tande and Claire hurried out toward them, breathless and with more than a little fear on their faces.

"Oh my gosh, DJ, I'm so sorry about the cake." Claire started to ramble as soon as they were within earshot. "I was so sure that the cake was really a frosted pile of horse crap that I made Aidan take a piece. I just didn't think to tell him not to take it from the bottom."

Claire had made her fiancé eat sabotaged cake? That image was enough to push DJ over the edge. She looked up at Brent, who apparently was thinking the same thing. Their snickers turned into full out laughs until she and Brent were holding each other up, tears streaming down their faces.

"Oh my God," Brent gasped. "Please, please tell me that the cake was actually pink frosted horse shit and that Aidan actually did eat it."

DJ had a hard time catching her breath. The damn dress fit like a corset. "Oh my God, can you imagine his face? Priceless. That would be worth a thousand wedding cakes."

"Well, I'm glad you're finding at least some of this funny and no, your cake was just cake. Though he did say it was actually quite good. Here, I saved you some." Claire held up a small round tier that still had the little bride and groom, though a bit lopsided, on top.

Brent took his finger and tasted the frosting. "Hmmm, not bad." He took the cake and held some out to DJ. "Come on, take a bite."

DJ raised an eyebrow, not at all trusting the expression on his face. "You wouldn't be thinking of doing anything crazy, now would you?"

"Baby, I married you didn't I?"

She gasped and Brent took the opportunity to give her a *big* bite. Frosting smeared across her mouth. Not one to waste an opportunity, she licked her lips. "Pretty tasty. Now your turn," she said, grinning at Brent through layers of pink.

He didn't even finish shaking his head before the entire cake found his face.

Tande tried to cover her bark of laughter with her hand, but it was too late.

DJ didn't even look her way, just swiped some cake off her husband's face and pushed it into Tande's.

What ensued was a full out food fight that only ended when all four of them were covered in sticky icing and laughing so hysterically, that for years afterwards Claire was likely going to have to deny being drunk.

"Hey, look," Brent said, grabbing DJ and pointing to the sky. Bright blasts of purple and red and pink fireworks filled the night.

Sighs of *ooohhs* and *ahhhhs* came from the guests behind them, while DJ squealed in delight.

DJ stood and watched the night fill with beautiful colors, one after another. She turned to her husband. "Did you do this?"

He smiled, but gave her a non-committal shrug. Just then a huge pink heart burst into the air with the initials DK + BK firmly in the center.

She watched the sparks fall harmlessly to the ground, no longer bothered by her tears that fell with them. DJ turned to Brent and pulled his head down to hers. "I know the name of your new song."

"What?" he whispered against her mouth, giving her the taste of pink lemonade all over again.

"*Forever.*"

Then she kissed him.

About the Authors

Emma lives in Texas in a sprawling ranch style home with her husband, daughter, and a pack of rescue Bassett Hounds. She is an advocate for the American Society of Autism and does her part to spread awareness about the disorders associated with the Autism, sharing the experiences and trials she's experienced with her daughter.

Needless to say, life is never boring when you have an elementary-aged child and four or five 4-legged friends roaming the house. They keep her and her husband busy, smiling, and laughing.

Her stories reflect her love for the Lone Star State, sexy cowboys (she married one!), high-powered action, and romance.

P.S. She also writes paranormal romance as Krystal Shannan so if you need a little magick in your story, hop over and take a look.

RECEIVE A FREE NOVELLA WHEN YOU SIGN UP FOR EMMA'S NEWSLETTER!

KC Klein has lived most of her life with her head in the clouds and her nose buried in a book. She did stop reading long enough to make a home with a real life hero, her husband, for over sixteen years. A mother of two children, she spends her time slaying dragons, saving princesses, and championing the belief in the happily-ever-after. She's been a finalist in the 2012 Prism contest, been honored with a reviewer's choice award, and the 2012 RONE award for her sci-fi romance anthology.

KC loves to hear from readers and can be found desperately pounding away on her laptop in yoga pants and leopard slippers or more conveniently at www.kckleinbooks.com. Join her Rock Star Facebook Fan Group for updates on her latest releases, sales, and ARC giveaways.

Lavender lives in Texas with her own Prince Charming, two kids, two cats and a big brown rug-umm, dog. She spends her days writing sexy contemporary romances, sometimes adding a hint of suspense or tossing in a little dominance and submission. Lately, she's playing with a bit of magic, too. A member of RWA, she took first place in the Great Expectations

Contest in 2011 fpr Bound by Trust. When not writing or reading great romance novels, she can be found in the kitchen baking, usually with chocolate.

Jodi was born and raised in Mississippi. Her deep Southern roots and love of the paranormal led her to write Southern Paranormal novels. She currently lives in Northeast Arkansas with her handsome husband, brilliant son, a temperamental swan, and a yellow lab that is fond of retrieving turtles when duck season is over.

R.L. Syme is a best-selling, award-winning author of both contemporary and historical romance. After careers in youth work, musical theater, and non-profits, she writes Romantic Suspense, Medieval Historicals, and Young Adult fiction.

Her first novel, His Wounded Heart, was a finalist in the prestigious Genesis Award, the top honor for unpublished writers in the ACFW. Her first Highlander novel, The Outcast Highlander, was an Amazon best-seller, and the first volume of that series is now complete with Lachlan's Revenge. She is a member of Chick Tales--an author co-op that writes contemporary romance in Somewhere, TX.

Becca is a writer of heroes worth loving and villains worth hating. Lover of cheese (#fancycheese) and binge-watching and strawberries and hope. A Tweeter and Pinner of things. She loves to hear from readers via social media.

Chick Tales, LLC

http://chicktalesink.com

Find out more about Somewhere, TX at our website and subscribe to our blog to get updates on when you can expect the next volume to release.

Don't miss the free bonus novel, A MONTH OF SUNDAYS by R.L. Syme and Lavender Daye, as Joe Walker the bartender finds his unlikely match!

Recommend it.

Please help other readers find this book by recommending it to friends, readers' groups and discussion boards.

Review it.

Please tell other readers why you liked our books by reviewing them at Amazon or GoodReads.

Thank you!

www.ingramcontent.com/pod-product-compliance
Lightning Source LLC
Chambersburg PA
CBHW020548130626
46552CB00007B/2813